LOST ON ME

Also by Veronica Raimo

The Girl at the Door

VERONICA RAIMO

LOST ON ME

**TRANSLATED FROM THE ITALIAN BY
LEAH JANECZKO**

Black Cat
New York

First published in Italy in 2022 by Giulio Einaudi editore.

Published simultaneously in Canada
Printed in the United States of America

This book was translated thanks to a grant awarded by the Italian Ministry of
Foreign Affairs and International Cooperation.

The quotation in the epigraph is from Ursula K. Le Guin, "Indian Uncles," first
published in *The Wave in the Mind*, Shambhala Publications, 2004.

The quotations on pages 196 and 206 are from F. Scott Fitzgerald, *This Side of Paradise*.

This book was set in 12-pt. Minion Pro by Alpha Design & Composition of Pittsfield, NH.

First Grove Atlantic paperback edition: June 2023

Library of Congress Cataloging-in-Publication data is available for this title.

ISBN 978-0-8021-6204-5
eISBN 978-0-8021-6205-2

Black Cat
an imprint of Grove Atlantic
154 West 14th Street
New York, NY 10011

Distributed by Publishers Group West

groveatlantic.com

23 24 25 26   10 9 8 7 6 5 4 3 2 1

For Cecilia, Glenda, and Milena

Robert had introduced me to a very Yurok moral sentiment, shame. Not guilt, there was nothing to be guilty about; just shame. You blush resentfully, you hold your tongue, and you figure it out. I have Robert to thank in part for my deep respect for shame as a social instrument.

URSULA K. LE GUIN, "Indian Uncles"

*W*hen a writer is born into a family, the family is finished, they say.

Actually, the family will be just fine, as has always been the case since the dawn of time, while it's the writer who'll meet with a terrible fate in the desperate attempt to kill off mothers, fathers, and siblings only to once again find them inexorably alive.

My brother dies several times a month.

It's always my mother who phones to inform me of his passing.

"Your brother's not answering my calls," she says in a whisper.

To her, the telephone bears witness to our permanence on Earth, so if there's no answer, the only possible explanation is the cessation of all vital functions.

When she calls to tell me my brother is gone, she's not looking for reassurance. Instead she wants me to share in her grief. Suffering together is her form of happiness; misery shared is misery relished.

Sometimes the cause of death is banal: a gas leak, a head-on collision, a broken neck from a bad fall.

Other times the scenario is more complex.

My mother's call last Easter Monday was followed by another one from a young Carabiniere officer.

"Your mother has reported your brother's disappearance. Can you confirm this?"

They hadn't heard from each other for maybe a couple hours. He was out to lunch with his girlfriend, and she was agonizing over why he wasn't out to lunch with the person who'd brought him into this world.

I tried to reassure the young carabiniere. Everything was under control.

"No," he burst out, "everything is *not* under control. All hell has broken loose on our switchboard."

On that particular occasion my brother wasn't yet dead, but was at death's door. He was being held captive in a parking garage, having been kidnapped and tortured by henchmen sent out by the Italian Democratic Party. He'd recently become culture councillor of Rome's third municipal district, and at times there were disagreements with fellow party members.

"Don't bicker with anyone," my mother had warned him.

"Mamma, I don't bicker, I do politics."

"All right, just make up afterwards."

After ascertaining that her son is still alive, my mother always feels mortified. She pouts like a twelve-year-old girl. Her voice even turns into a twelve-year-old girl's. How can you get angry at a little girl?

"You think I should bring the carabinieri some pastries?" she asks in that little voice.

Come to think of it, who knows why she called the carabinieri and not the regular police? I don't dare pose the question, since it risks doubling the number of calls she'll make next time. The fire department, for example, or civil protection. She's never thought of them before.

When she's in a state of panic, my mother bargains with the Lord and imposes *fioretti* on herself: no eating sweets, no going to the movies, no reading magazines, no listening to Rai Radio 3, for weeks, months, years. These days she can't go to the hairdresser's or watch TV. Sometimes the combination is no Radio 3 and no sweets. Or no coffee and no new shoes. She mixes them, matches them—it depends.

I go over to see her because I'm worried.

"Ah, Verika, it's you." My mother calls me Verika. "I was hoping it was your brother."

She still lives in the apartment where I grew up, in a residential district in the northeast outskirts of Rome. The same district where her son has been made culture councillor. I wish I could convince her to convert at least one of her *fioretti* into a good deed. "Do a little volunteer work," I tell her. "I'm sure the Lord will approve."

She shakes her head, and as she does she asks me to turn on the TV and tell her what's going on in the world. Though she covers her eyes with her hands, I can see her peeking between her index and middle fingers. She gropes for the remote and turns up the volume. "Humph. You couldn't hear a thing."

While my brother was still being held hostage by the Democratic Party's thugs, my mother awaited the fatal phone call, trembling. "I vowed I would throw myself out the window."

"What a pleasant thought, Mamma. That way I'd have spent Easter Monday with my brother butchered and my mother splattered on the sidewalk."

Then a thought strikes me. "So, if they'd killed me instead, would you still have jumped?"

Silence.

She doesn't look at me because she still has one hand covering her eyes.

"Well? Would you have jumped?"

"Oh, don't ask silly questions."

When I get back home and think about it, there's something that doesn't add up in her near-suicide scenario: there isn't a single window in my parents' apartment that anyone could possibly jump out of. They're all too narrow, because they've been split in two.

My father had a fixation with dividing up rooms, for no reason at all. He would simply build a wall through them. He built walls in rooms—there's no other way to put it.

There were four of us living together in a sixty-square-meter apartment, which he'd managed to split up into three bedrooms, a living room, a kitchen, a dinette, a veranda, and two bathrooms, plus a long tunnel of overhead storage space that ran the full length of the apartment and lowered the ceiling. A particularly tall person would've banged their head against it, but no one in our family had that problem.

There were no real doors to speak of—just sliding panels without locks. It was like living on a theater set: the rooms were purely symbolic, simulations for the benefit of spectators.

For part of my childhood, my bedroom existed only at night. During the day it became a hallway again. When it was time to go to sleep, I would close two folding doors and pull down a section of the wall that was actually a Murphy bed. In the morning it all disappeared; the set was changed. Panels were slid back, curtains raised. Later, my bedroom was moved into my brother's, a tiny rectangle squeezed into one corner of the room like a horizontally positioned broom closet. The window—like all the others—was bisected by the wall. If I wanted to look out at the world, I had to make do with an opening as wide as a minibar door.

"*Just so you know, you wouldn't have fit through the window,*" I write to my mother.

"*Thank you, dear,*" she replies. "*I'll keep that in mind.*"

I learned to read at age four. In another family that might have earned me at least one "Brava!" In my family it was utterly irrelevant, given that my brother had learned to read at around three, and by four he'd memorized all the world capitals, the inauguration dates of all the American presidents in chronological order, and the names of all the Juventus players dating back to 1975, the year he was born.

In terms of the distribution of roles, the fact that he'd nabbed that of family genius actually made my life a whole lot easier. My mother claims that, when given the chance to start school a year early like my brother did, I replied, "No thank you, Mamma. I want to be like everyone else."

I doubt that at age five I had the wherewithal to utter anything of the sort, but it's true that, in some ways, I was in the position of not needing to prove anything to anyone. For my brother, things weren't so easy. I didn't envy him.

There's an anecdote my mother always tells. Once, at a restaurant—before he was even three—he picked up the menu and began to recite it from the pulpit of his high chair. He used syntactic doubling, intuited all the diaereses, and prolonged the right consonants. The server who'd come to take the order just stood there, an annoyed look on his face, waiting for the snotty kid to finish his *récitation*. When my brother reached the end of the dessert list, the server continued to stand there, pen in hand, not looking the least bit impressed.

"So, you ready to order or should I come back?"

At this reaction, the little genius was so overcome with frustration that he grabbed a glass off the table and bit into it.

My mother is always so proud when she tells this anecdote, and, just like her three-year-old son, she gets upset if someone hearing it doesn't look amused enough, driving her to tell the story all over again so she can explain the key points.

When my mother introduced us to new people, she would say, "These are my jewels." Not all jewels are alike, though. After she listed off the amazing things my brother could do—poetic octonaries extolling the feats of Garibaldi, equations involving two unknowns, diagramless backwards crossword puzzles, rounds of Mastermind solved in three moves—it was my turn. "And Verika likes to draw," she would say. The end.

It wasn't even true, but given my lack of exceptional brilliance, it had been decided that I wasn't half bad at drawing. Even nonno Peppino, my father's father, played a part in constructing this persona. When I was little, the only game I liked playing in the weekly puzzle magazine *La Settimana Enigmistica* was an activity called *I Drew This*. It consisted of drawing a picture starting from a few lines they'd printed inside a frame. One time I drew a sort of alien, which my grandpa mistook for a cat and labeled *The Curious Cat*. A month later he handed me an illustrated book of La Fontaine's fables, saying it was a prize that *La Settimana Enigmistica* had sent for my curious cat. Even back then I knew he was blatantly lying, because I'd already checked the winning drawings and there was no sign of my alien passed off as a cat.

Still, I was happy with the present, and above all I ended up convinced that if my grandpa could lie, well, all the more reason that I could too. And so, one day, at the middle school where my mother worked, as I waited for her to finish a faculty meeting, I snuck into an empty classroom where oil paintings had been left to dry beneath the students' desks. I was in third grade. These were pictures by eighth graders. I inspected them one by one, smudging my little fingerprints on their edges, then decided to steal a stormy sea and a snow-covered cabin. I waved the pages in the air for a good ten minutes, blowing on them, and slid them into my book bag.

My father had given me a tempera painting kit, and one Sunday afternoon I decided to stage my little act. After lunch I shut myself up in my room, pretending to be in a creative frenzy. I reemerged hours later with my two masterpieces. No one took any notice of the fact that they were already dry, or that they were done with oils and not tempera paints, or even that on the back of each of them was a name crossed out with a blue ballpoint pen.

My parents were so enthusiastic about the two paintings—which would be the only ones of my career—that they decided to frame them and hang them in our hallway.

When guests came over, the guided tour always included the art gallery in the hallway, and amid all the compliments showered on the tenebrous depths of the tempestuous sea and the romantic solitude of the mountainside haven, I ended up convincing myself I really could claim part of the credit. I was the one who'd decided which paintings to steal. I hadn't let myself be beguiled by simple line art or childish brushstrokes, much less by trite portraits of happy families, leafy trees, bucolic landscapes. Despite my tender age, for me, nothing less than Sturm und Drang would do.

The two paintings still hang in my mother's hallway. When I go to visit her and I walk by them, I'm tempted to tell her the truth. I'm afraid she wouldn't believe me, though. My rare attempts to be honest with her are never taken seriously, and are instead viewed with a mix of suspicion and pity. If she notices I'm upset around the paintings, she comes over and gives me a little stroke on the head, as if I were once again the little girl who made them, though that girl is not me.

"Want Mamma to buy you a canvas?" she asks.

At times I imagine that evidence of my crime as an eight-year-old might emerge like in a horror story, that the

mountain cabin's immaculate snowy mantle might become
stained with blue ink. Other times I tell myself I should take
back the paintings, remove them from the frames and try to
decipher the names on the back of them, look the people up
on Facebook, offer my apologies thirty years after the fact,
write a long letter in the form of a novel:

> *Dearest artists,*
>
> *Forgive me, I beseech you. Who knows what a
> turn your lives must have taken, and who knows
> what despair you must have endured that morn-
> ing when you entered the classroom, your eyes
> still groggy from slumber, and slid your gifted
> hand beneath the desk only to find your paint-
> ings gone. A collision with the void! The cosmic
> breach of trust! Oh, that my deception led to oth-
> ers leaves me in anguish. Whatever did you tell
> your art teacher? "We're sorry, ma'am. Someone
> has stolen our pictures"? Were you believed or
> ridiculed? I can only imagine the entire class-
> room's derision, the childish cruelty with which it
> humiliated its finest prodigies. Such suffering is a
> torment to me . . .*

Actually, a second later I stop thinking about it.

My brother and I both became writers. I don't know what he answers when people ask him why that is. I say it's thanks to all the boredom our parents imparted to us.

While my mother had high anxiety, my father had a subtler form of paranoia. His chemistry studies made him see the world as a petri dish of harmful substances we constantly needed to protect ourselves from. This meant leaving the house as little as possible, suffocating within four walls—or, in our case, a hundred.

I was eight at the time of the nuclear reactor meltdown in Chernobyl. Even when the emergency seemed to be over, my family continued to exist in a postapocalyptic film scenario, pretending we lived not in a relatively well-off city in the Western world, but in a sci-fi Zone X with high levels of contamination.

In every respectable catastrophe story, when the world's been infected, all that matters is preserving one's blood ties: the family. And so for three years my father didn't let us eat fruits, vegetables, or eggs, or drink milk, or go out to restaurants, or buy pizza from street vendors. The only foods allowed were canned goods dated before April 26, 1986.

It wasn't easy to follow this protocol, but I must confess that it made things interesting, made me feel like a heroine living in a state of quarantine invisible to the rest of the world. Staying entrenched in our secure apartment, eating tuna and beans like the pioneers, coming up with outlandish excuses to turn down a snack when studying at a classmate's, or checking the packaging dates at the supermarket as though they were secret codes meant just for us, the chosen few.

We all ended up with a pretty bad vitamin deficiency, and though my mother drugged us with Be-Total and Co-Carnetina, we were all a bit green around the gills. Still, we survived. Worst-case scenario, we risked coming down with scurvy.

Thanks to our strict upbringing, neither my brother nor I ever learned to do such hazardous things as swimming, riding a bike, skating, or jumping rope (in a flash we might have drowned, cracked our skulls, broken a leg, strangled ourselves).

We spent our childhood cooped up at home, bored off our asses. It was such an all-consuming activity that it soon became an existential pose. We knew how to be bored like nobody's business.

In our building there were always kids playing down in the courtyard, and their shouts and cries reached our ears like some strange animal language we didn't understand. We would spy on them from our sliver of a window, in silence, the lights out. We would take turns raising our faces a few centimeters above the windowsill (there wasn't room for us both) to then duck down if one of the kids looked up as they followed the arc of a ball sailing through the air. We were terrified by the thought that they might see us, because we wouldn't have known how to handle an invitation to join them. Two little spies barricaded inside their home.

The worst part is we never even saw ourselves that way. I mean, we could've turned it into a game—"Ha! They didn't see us!"—enjoyed the thrill of not getting caught, debating who was the cutest boy or girl in the group, at least as much listless diversion as old men staring at a construction site. But no, not even that. We were just two kids who were really good at being bored off their asses.

One day, from the secrecy of our hiding place, we faced an appalling moral dilemma. The kids in the courtyard were playing soccer with a toad. At first the animal was simply placed in the middle of them all, surrounded, like the typical loser in an episode of adolescent bullying. The toad hazarded a couple leaps, but it clearly had no escape plan. Then, from the circle of legs, the first kick swung out. They started dribbling it to one another. What reached our outpost were more the idiotic little shouts of humans than the thump of a shoe making impact against the creature's warty flesh, or the

splat of its body against the asphalt when someone missed
a pass, but in my head it was all loud and clear. My brother
and I squeezed each other's hands throughout that endless
torment. I think he was praying. I could hear him mumbling
litanies, though he didn't make the sign of the cross because
I wouldn't let go of his hand. I just wished the toad would die
quickly and put us out of our misery. We couldn't breathe. Or
better, we deliberately chose not to. Cowardly and hopeless,
as always. So was that what our parents were trying to protect
us from? The discovery of evil in our own courtyard? The
horror, the horror!

When we finally discovered books, it wasn't a form of es-
capism, but rather the reassuring coalescence of boredom. I
could almost picture it in my mind, white and miry: reading
was like sinking into a pool of milk. I would stay immersed
for hours, until even my body grew flaccid, the stagnant
liquid seeping into my pores. It felt like everything suddenly
acquired meaning, a phenomenon of transubstantiation, my
flesh changing into boredom. I couldn't say whether I liked
a book. That was never the point. In fact, I imagined that
attempting to derive any pleasure from reading would have
been a lost cause. Why bother trying? Besides, there was one
thing my family feared even more than the toxic cloud from
Chernobyl: hedonism.

B efore books came along to dope us with boredom, my brother and I came up with other pastimes.

The family genius had invented a game that took up our afternoons for several summers. From right after lunchtime until the sun went down, and up to the point when we needed to go have dinner, we would lie on the floor side by side, propped up on our elbows with a notebook in front of us to play the numbers challenge. We didn't play against each other but beside each other, because the game wasn't competitive. Actually it wasn't collaborative either. It was more like the Zen exercise of counting sheep jumping over a fence when you were trying to fall asleep. You rolled a die and marked down the number that turned up. We spent hours doing it. Committed, engrossed. We were both big fans of five, so the only real highlight of the game was hoping the five turned up as often as possible. Which showed its superiority. As I rolled my die, I would peek at my brother rolling his, would sense in his focused gaze the hope that it would be a five, followed his steady, honest hand marking an X below the number four. Barely a glimmer of regret in his eyes and then, with perfect faith, ready for the next roll. Careful not to be seen, I would mark an X in my notebook below the five, lowering a curtain of fingers in front of my die, which had landed on a pitiful two. I was capable of cheating at a Zen game. It was senseless. Still, I couldn't help it.

When my parents called us to dinner and he and I compared notes, my five always came out the winner. I don't know if my brother knew I was cheating, or if he couldn't even have fathomed anything so petty. He tried to decipher the data and was surprised at how it defied all statistical probability. He tried to discern another possible logical explanation, attempted his first forays into metaphysics. How could I have rolled a five so many times? Then he would pat me on the back and say, "Brava."

I've often thought about that "brava." I've wondered whether it was due to the principle of communicating vessels, whether my brother needed to force out a "brava" or two every so often to make room for all the others being directed at him. I've also wondered if it was one of his first manifestations of sarcasm. Involuntary, perhaps. I've wondered whether he actually wanted to tell me "brava" to praise my silly trick, my attempt to overcome the boredom of his inane game by doing something even more inane. Whether he was trying to say to me: how can we escape this bedroom? How can we break free?

Actually, that's what I've been doing my whole life. Whenever I feel like I'm trapped in a room, in a game with rules, rather than trying to escape from it I try to taint the logic of the room, of the rules. To imagine things that aren't true, to say them, cause them, until I believe them. Until I believe a die can always turn up five, even though it makes absolutely no difference at all.

As a teenager I tried to break free from the rules of my room by running away from home. My plan immediately came up against our apartment's spatial arrangement. I'd packed a suitcase for my escape, a nice small one, barely more than a bundle, but it was still too bulky to pass through the measly sliver to which my bedroom window had been reduced. And so I sorted my belongings into three plastic bags and tossed them down to the ground below. Then I told my parents I was going out for gelato.

Still today, given how my escape turned out, when I find myself eating gelato with my mother—or letting her lick half of mine because it's one of her current *fioretti* ("The Lord won't be upset if I have one taste")—she can't wait to drag up the old story: "You were so cute, with your adolescent tantrums."

Before throwing my clothes and a couple books out the window, I'd stolen a million two hundred thousand liras in cash from my father's dresser. He kept his money tucked neatly beneath his rolled-up belt, his comb, and a cork he would singe and then daub his mustache with to cover the gray whiskers.

I invested the first thirty thousand liras in buying myself a backpack and dumped the contents of the plastic bags into it. My medium-term plan was to catch a train to Paris the next day. I didn't have an address to go to, or a friend there, just a history of watching too many French films, thanks to which I hoped to recognize the coolest cafés.

My short-term plan was to take the train to Fiumicino Airport so I could say goodbye to Za—the boy I was dating—who was leaving for Ireland. This was back when Ireland was all the rage and spending three weeks surrounded by drab little towns, the countryside, drizzle, dark beer, and shitty music seemed like something to experience.

It was the first real goodbye in my life. To be perfectly honest, I'd been building up to that moment in my mind since the day we started going out. In fact, I think that was exactly why I started dating him in the first place: so we could leave each other. The thought that he'd be leaving the country soon ensured me a misery I could enjoy without the hassle of having to go out and find one myself.

In the run-up to his departure I'd gone to bed crying every night. I was fifteen.

I'd had no choice but to run away from home because my parents wanted to keep me from experiencing the tragic farewell I'd been yearning for for months. It turned out that Za's flight was leaving on nonno Peppino's birthday. We were supposed to go over to his place for lunch, and they didn't think I had a good enough reason to justify my skipping out on it.

When I got to Fiumicino, Za flashed me an ambiguous smile as though he were trying to pick me up. Then he realized it was me.

"The fuck are you doing here?"

Slung over his shoulders was the guitar he was going to play on the streets of Dublin to scrape together spending money for the trip. On his head, a hat for collections. In his pocket, a book of Bob Dylan lyrics.

Anyway, I made my little scene. I was happy, I was sad, everything went just as planned.

"Whoa, you realize this girl ran away from home for you?" asked the friend who was leaving with him, pulling the price tag off my backpack, and only then did I see in Za's eyes something I mistook for a feeling of tenderness. Something that more likely was panic.

Part Two of my escape plan, before taking the train to Paris the next day, was a night at the home of Ernesto, a guy who worked at the *gelateria*. He was the only person I knew who had his own place, because he was twenty-four.

Me and Cecilia, my best friend—at the time, the expression had ontological significance—used to go to his place to buy weed and read his comic books. He was kind of like an older brother or a wayward uncle. He'd never hit on either of us. And we, though never admitting it, were both hurt by this.

I have no idea why he didn't get bored hanging out with two teenaged girls who were crazy about *Beverly Hills, 90210* and Proust, girls he didn't want to make a move on. Maybe he was simply too stoned to care.

Not only was Cecilia my best friend, but she'd also become my role model on the first day of high school, when she sat at the desk in front of mine. She was a lot taller than me, drew a lot better than me, and above all had read more books, which was a first among the other kids my age. Rather than hurting my pride, my being outdone in that category finally redeemed books in my eyes, since I'd always dismissed them as a quagmire of boredom, a family monopoly.

Cecilia didn't read only the books she found around her house, didn't endure them as a form of forced inheritance— she bought them too. She'd already developed her own personal taste, and she was the one who, for example, made me discover Philip Roth.

I showed up at Ernesto's with my backpack on my back. I told him I'd been locked out of my apartment, my folks were out of town, and the next day I had to catch the train to Paris. Could I stay the night?

I don't know if he followed everything I said, but he nodded and went back to rolling a joint, even though he already had one tucked behind his ear.

"You can take a shower if you want," he told me.

"I don't need one, thanks."

"You need one. Trust me."

Rome's hundred-degree August weather, the adrenaline of running away, stealing from my father, the emotion of the farewell, and my adolescent hormones were making themselves known. My body was emanating all the smells of that day, ever since breakfast at my parents' home, when I was still a daughter plotting my days ahead with a silent snicker, winking at my brother, who had no idea why, choosing the right books to take along, will five pairs of underwear be enough? Only pants, or a dress too? A final farewell to Klaus Kinski, who made all my girlfriends ask why I had a picture of my grandpa hanging on the wall when they came over, and then swift, determined strides, my mature mask, my heartbeat nearly giving me away but my voice remaining firm when announcing, "I'm going out for some gelato." Yes, it had been an important day and I didn't want to part with its smells.

Having spent an hour of my freedom reading Mr. Natural comics on Ernesto's sofa, I struck useless Lolita poses as he puttered around the apartment in his underwear and watered dead flowers on the balcony from a beer bottle. Then the phone rang. Ernesto went to answer it and came back to me.

"It's your dad."

"I don't want to talk to him."

"Looks like you have to. He wants to report me for abducting a minor."

On the phone my father bluffed brilliantly. Told me he just wanted to talk, and then I'd be free to do whatever I wanted. I fell for it hook, line, and sinker. Go to Paris? Sure, why not? Even Lisbon! Helsinki!

"Call your grandpa, though. He's furious."

Ernesto gave me a matchbox with a couple joints in it to help me get through the night. "Hey, sorry, I'm just not up for going to the slammer."

I gave him a peck on the cheek to express my affection and my us-against-them solidarity, even though I was the one heading back to prison. He laid his hand on my waist, pulling me closer. Then he hesitated, as though momentarily gripped by an urge that had already subsided.

Minutes later I heard my father talking to him over the intercom, addressing him as "sir."

The last part of my escape saw me sitting in a diner with the whole family, silently eating rubbery pizza. My father made me pay for it and then hand over the rest of his money. When we got back home, with an innocent smile my mother told me, "He'll call you tomorrow. I know he will."

She was talking about Za. He was the one who ratted me out.

Just as his plane was about to take off, there was an on-board announcement: "Attention, all passengers. A minor has been reported missing." Then they said my name. Za was escorted off the plane and taken over to a phone to talk to my mother. He told her everything. He even named names: Ernesto, the guy from the *gelateria*, though he didn't know his last name. And with this, all my dreams of making a new life for myself in Paris were shattered.

Thinking back on it now, I wonder why my plan never included me going to Ireland with him. I simply hadn't considered it. Which was a good thing, since he was going there to stay with Anastasia, who was on a study-abroad trip in Ireland, in an apartment paid for by her parents. But I would find that out later.

I spent my August holed up in my room staring at that sliver of a window from which it would've been impossible to jump and waiting for a phone call that never came. My brother looked at me with pity, Klaus Kinski stared at me sternly.

When three weeks had passed, I came out of isolation to go to the phone and call Za's place.

He had six brothers. All seven of them spoke with a weak *R* and had nicknames whose origins were shrouded

in mystery: Uomme, Tippe, Cro . . . and he, of course, was
Za. I'd been rebaptized Smilzi. The first call came to nothing. Someone speaking with a weak *R* informed me that Za
wasn't home.

"Could you tell him I called?"

"Yeah, sure."

Nobody called me back.

Over the next few days I continued to call and interact
with Za's brothers, who answered with Za's voice to tell me
he wasn't there. I became paranoid that it was Za answering,
telling me that sure, he'd let him know I called.

"Uomme, it's Smilzi. Is Za there?"

"No, sorry."

"Can you tell him I called?"

"Yeah, sure."

"Uomme, tell me the truth: is that you, Za?"

"No, this is Cro."

After a week I gave up. I took down Klaus Kinski's picture because I couldn't stand his judgmental stare anymore.
Fortunately the nightmare of August was over. September
seemed like a far more dignified month to start to live again.
I ran into Za a few days later at the Festa de l'Unità. He had
his arm around a blond girl with curls that coiled down like
streamers and a nose so tiny it looked fake. Which it was.
He introduced her to me: "Anastasia."

I said my name.

"Oh, so you're the one who ran away. You had us really worried."

I stared at her dark roots.

During his three weeks in Ireland, Za never once got in touch with me, but he'd heard from my mother. It seems she'd called to reassure him that I was safe and sound at home. I was holed up in the two square meters of my bedroom, crying all day, banging my head against the walls, and had stopped eating, but was nevertheless safe and sound.

I have no idea how my mother managed to track down the phone number of Anastasia's apartment in Dublin, but I've stopped wondering about her investigative skills. A few years later, when I was hanging out with Cecilia and our friends Glenda and Milena in a giant hot tub at a party with perfect strangers we'd picked up off the street, the bathroom door burst open. "Francesca's on the phone," said a dazed-looking guy as he tested the temperature of the water. It was two a.m. My girlfriends and I and a couple other just-as-random girls who were splashing around in the coconut-scented bubble bath all stared at each other, trying to figure out what to make of the statement. Was it a coded message that only the cleverest of us could decipher? A password announcing the second act of the evening? But then he added, "Says she's Verika's mother."

Half an hour later my father was downstairs in the car, waiting to drive me and my friends home. I plopped into the front seat while they squeezed into the back. I could sense their bodies behind me, emanating anger and coconut. It took me almost a month to win back their friendship.

But from then on, "Francesca's on the phone" actually did become our coded message for when we sensed one of us was doing something really stupid.

It was the line we used for rejecting boyfriends who didn't seem good enough ("Hmm . . . Cute face, but Francesca's on the phone"), jeans that fit too tight ("Your ass looks great, but Francesca's on the phone"), a warning that one of us was about to pass out ("Come on, gimme the joint, Francesca's on the phone"). If we wanted to rent a porno video, we'd say, "How about a nice little movie that'll get Francesca on the phone?"

In any case, Francesca was always on the phone.

During college I started going out with one of my brother's friends, for reasons that were more practical than sentimental. I was constantly searching for ways to escape from home but was too lazy to find a job and earn enough to rent a room. The thought of escape is always exciting; going about it, not as much.

Loris, my brother's friend, worked for a newspaper and lived in a little penthouse in Monteverde that he'd inherited from his grandmother. The apartment was tiny and had a ridiculously big four-poster bed that took up half the space, but it was his grandmother's bed, so he kept it. Then came the second major obstacle in his place: me. And for a while he kept that too.

I moved in with him less than a week after we started dating, which maybe should've made him suspicious, but it all happened before he even knew what hit him. One day I showed up on his doorstep, suitcase in hand. He thought I wanted to stay for the weekend.

"No, for my whole life," I said. My romanticism always has a touch of the foreboding.

While my goal was to get out of my parents' place, I have no idea what Loris's was. It was like he decided to adopt a daughter who was already of age and already bored. When he got home from staff meetings, he'd look around in disbelief at the mess I'd managed to make in just a couple hours. He was convinced my messiness was an indictment of his inherited penthouse, which contradicted his self-proclaimed status as a member of the proletariat. Actually, it was nothing but me being lazy.

Loris was a guy who would turn the Clash up full blast at home, pretending to mosh with invisible creatures, and then blow a fuse if someone rearranged the pens lined up on his desk. Our relationship ended when I started putting my cigarettes out on his ripe peaches. (I only ate unripe fruit.)

One night, before our brief cohabitation was over, Loris and I were fucking in his four-poster bed. It must've been around eight, and the landline started ringing off the hook. Loris kept focusing on what his dick was doing until it became impossible to ignore the obsessive trill. He got up to answer. Francesca was on the phone.

"Is my son there?"

Not only does my mother never say hello, but she skips the whole package of useless pleasantries—"How are you?", "Is this a bad time?", "What are you doing?"—and gets straight to the point.

"No, Francesca. Sorry."

"What on earth could he be doing at this time of night?"

"I don't know, Francesca. Maybe he's fucking, just like I was until a second ago."

Though he was turned away from me, I could picture the smirk on Loris's face, him all proud of his scathing comeback, which compensated for the neatly aligned pens on his desk.

My mother wasn't about to be intimidated. "I don't understand you kids. Is it too much to ask that you call your mothers before you start fucking?"

Loris came back to bed with his dick demoralized, and a week later he used the peaches as an excuse to mercilessly send me back to live with Francesca.

Luckily, my mother took it upon herself to avenge me. She kept calling Loris to find out where my brother and I were, even after he'd thrown me out of the penthouse. And he knew better than to try to outsmart her by ignoring the phone, because she wouldn't have thought twice before assailing the newspaper's editorial staff.

My brother and I owed our friends a debt of gratitude: hanging out with us meant being bombarded with phone calls from my mother day and night. Not only did she call anyone who had even a tenuous relationship with her children to constantly monitor their permanence on Earth, but after having tracked us down, she also made a second round of calls to thank everyone for their help and assure them everything was perfectly fine.

While her anxiousness for my brother still today drives her to dream up Argentinean desaparecido-like scenarios, the kind she feels for me is never tinged with the heroic, but rather with the erotic. In her eyes, no one has any intention of doing me harm, but simply of doing me.

My mother has never slept with anyone but my father, not only before they started dating, but also in all their years of marriage and after his death. I have no proof of this, but I tend to believe her. She's never taken a taxi once in her life, because she's convinced that any taxi driver might turn out to be a maniac and take her who knows where. When she goes to mass, she says she feels the congregation of widowers leering at her. The boys who ask her for a euro to help carry her groceries are clearly trying to touch her ass. And what about the little grin the butcher flashes her when slipping sausages into her bag, or the greengrocer when insisting on gifting her a few bananas (though she accepts the bananas, because they're free)?

"All men are lecherous," she's always telling me.

When I was little, that word—"lecherous"—frightened me. It seemed slimy, greasy. I didn't understand what it meant, but the sound of it was spine-chilling.

The King of the Lechers was a colleague of hers back then, a technical education teacher, a stocky, mustachioed man who was always a bit short of breath. He sweat a lot, and would wipe his bald head with his shirtsleeve, but apart from that he was just an ordinary guy. My mother never missed the chance to remind me how lecherous he was. She would whip out that word and I would be terrified.

I was still going to elementary school and spent the whole day there. My mother taught at the middle school and in the afternoons held a theater workshop with her students, feeling like Giorgio Strehler. That year she was putting on a production of Pirandello's *The Oil Jar*. I wasn't allowed to go home alone after school, so I had no choice but to wait in my school courtyard for her to come pick me up in her VW Bug.

I'd grown to enjoy that lonely downtime. It became part of me. A fundamental part. During those hours I was Veronika, a pop star perpetually on world tour who met new men day after day and then abandoned them, ready to set off for her next destination. I knew nothing about sex, so her encounters were never consummated in bed but were limited to heart-wrenching farewells, teary eyes, and *I-love-yous* whispered into ears or shouted into the wind.

I would lean back against the school gate and blather to myself, sign autographs, receive mountains of fan mail, do sound checks in front of the empty stadium, and wait for my mother to arrive, honking her horn from a kilometer away.

One day I waited until six o'clock and she didn't show. The janitor had to lock the gate. Veronika was performing in Toronto in a skintight white latex dress when who should pull up in his little Fiat Panda but the King of the Lechers. My mother had decided to become the costume designer too and was racking her brains trying to dress up one little boy as an oil jar and two others as halves of an oil jar.

I'd always been given strict instructions never to accept—for any reason whatsoever—car rides, and now the King of the Lechers himself was telling me to get into his car so he could drop me off with my mother at her school. I started sweating even more than he was. I was in agony. I didn't know who to obey: my mother with her admonitions, or the King of the Lechers with his authority as an adult?

Fearfully, I opened the car door and huddled up on the back seat. The King of the Lechers asked me the typical questions people ask little kids: "What'd you do in school today?", "Are you hungry?", "Want some ice cream?" I flattened myself against the backrest, wondering if that was the King of the Lechers' actual strategy: forcing me to answer him. I remembered my mother's warnings: don't speak to strangers. Was he a stranger? I decided to keep quiet.

He didn't give up. "Cat got your tongue? Want me to roll up my window?" Nothing. I wouldn't give in. "You sure are a shy little girl, aren't you?" The insinuation struck home. It was then that the first trickle began to creep out, until I found myself sopping wet. I was so scared, I'd peed myself. My underwear was drenched, as were my pants, the seat, even the floor mat.

When we pulled up at my mother's school, I didn't want to get out. The King of the Lechers stared at me, not understanding. He seemed sweet, caring. "What's wrong?" I kept quiet. Then, finally, he ran out of patience. "Listen, little girl, I have things to do." At this, he got out and opened my door to find himself facing that sad spectacle.

He told me to wait in the car and went into the school to borrow a hair dryer from the janitor. He took me into the bathroom at a café and dried me off in front, then made me rest my hands on the wall and dried me off behind. He used it to dry his bald head too, maybe to spare his shirtsleeve. Then he left me with the hair dryer so I could return it. But I was so ashamed that I dumped it in a garbage can before

walking into the school and hurrying down the hallway toward the auditorium.

My mother was still there, grappling with the oil jars. I sat
down in the back row with my hands on my lap to cover up
the stain on my pants.

I wondered if that was what the word "lecher" meant: a
grown-up man who dries off your private parts in a café
bathroom. Should I tell my mother? What would happen?
Everything considered, her colleague had been kind, had
done it with good intentions.

An hour earlier I'd been a world-famous pop star, and
now I'd gone back to being a little girl who'd peed her pants.
I decided to protect both myself and the King of the Lechers.
To keep that embarrassing moment a secret, like a discovery
that was all mine. I took my hands off my lap and crossed
my legs for the first time in my life.

My moments of deepest solitude have been spent on the toilet.

Ever since I was a little girl, going to the bathroom has been an agonizing experience. I had to face up to my incapability with a boundless sense of expectation that might not lead anywhere. It was my apprenticeship in frustration.

Those who've never been constipated can't understand the exasperating torment of those endless minutes, the slow descent into the desolation of empty time, the longing to surrender.

Failure isn't the worst thing about it; the worst thing is the uncertainty, the precariousness.

There's part of you that can't let go, and yet it no longer belongs to you.

Your body pushes in opposite directions. First it tries to free itself, contracts to leverage on that single center of tension, then, weary, it reverses its efforts, tries to reopen, yielding, to draw back into it the tiny newborn head. The thing is, by then it's impossible for it to do either. Your brain sends out contradictory impulses. You wish you had another brain that controlled the first, that it would tell it either to stop or to try to work in just one direction, to the point of exhaustion. Instead, exhaustion is the middle ground.

I've spent countless hours in that deadlock. Desperate. Hopeless. Me, alone on the toilet, unable to get up. Abandoned by the world.

Sometimes I hear writers talk about their sense of despair when staring at a blank page. Naturally, that happens to me too, though no matter how humiliating it might be, there's always something so heroic in that image—the sense of a challenge, faith in the creative act that will make up for everything. My despair was different.

The only one who sensed my intimate suffering was nonno Peppino. When I was little, he would wait half an hour for me to leave the bathroom. When I didn't emerge, he would come in. He would crouch down in front of me and squeeze my little hands, stare at me for a long time, hypnotically. He had implacable blue eyes, which on those occasions sweetened.

"Okay, Scarafona, come on! Push, push . . ."

He called me Scarafona. Little Roach.

I pushed, gave it my all. He kept squeezing my hands and talking to me gently. "Come on, it's coming out, keep going."

"I can't!"

"Sure you can."

I had to do it, for him.

I tried again. Pushed. Hand in hand.

"You can do it." His voice steady and reassuring. It pained me to even think of letting him down. All the same, I couldn't do it. I tried to pull it back in. My grandpa noticed and squeezed my hands tighter. "Scarafona, don't give up. You're almost there."

I felt like crying. It must have been torture for him too, seeing a little girl so battered by life, but with a clear-eyed gaze he continued to instill me with confidence.

Then he tried using a distraction. Maybe if I focused on something else my intestine would feel less under pressure. He laid *La Settimana Enigmistica* on my lap and taught me to solve the rebus puzzles. The pictures fascinated me. They were the sacred art of a deeper universe where every single element brimmed with meaning. I got lost in them.

The deadlock didn't end. He solved the rebus puzzles before my admiring eyes, then dropped the pen and went back to squeezing my hands. "Let's try again."

After another half hour, he gave up.

He let go of my hands, and the forced evacuation began. Then we both scrubbed our hands clean and tried to forget the whole episode.

My grandpa often told me that during the war, a fellow soldier once mistook a dog turd for a piece of stale bread and ate it. After a few bites he realized his mistake, but maintained a certain aplomb: "Actually, everything considered, it's not half bad."

With these anecdotes, he wasn't trying to tell me about the brutality of war, about hardships or humiliations I hadn't experienced. Instead, it was a way to lecture me on a fundamental ethical principle: there's nothing so disgusting as our own disgust.

No one else has ever been there to squeeze my hands as I agonize on the toilet. It's not an easy thing to ask for. I've been left only with a sense of solitude and inadequacy. Whenever I'm up against the affliction, I begin to reinterpret my whole life as follows: it's a constant battle between abandoning something and trying to take it back. The perpetual curse of the middle ground.

Once, when in Sardinia to present one of my novels, I had the terrible idea of trying to go to the bathroom an hour before the event.

Forty minutes later I was still there, writhing and sweating, bracing my legs against the floor, my arms against the wall, doubling over. Nothing doing.

They started calling me on my cell phone, then someone came knocking on my hotel room door. I didn't answer. I had around ten minutes before I needed to either show my face or come up with an excuse. Like I always did. So many creative truths concocted to cover up for my shortcomings. A chlorine allergy if someone invited me to the pool, or an autoimmune disease that kept me from exposing myself to sunlight just to get out of going to the beach with friends, all because I couldn't swim.

I wept. How I missed my grandpa. I tried using his method. My phone continued to ring. More frantic pounding on my door. Once the mission was accomplished, I used up the whole tiny bottle of shower gel to wash my hands. I picked up the phone and called them back. "God, I'm sorry. I fell asleep."

The excuse came to me naturally: I suffered from a crippling form of narcolepsy.

"It started happening years ago. Just like that, all of a sudden I fall asleep. *Boom.* Out cold."

Concern and alarm among those present. What's important is never the believability, just the self-delusion. I end up convincing myself it's not a lie. There's a version of my life in which I really do suffer from crippling narcolepsy. I promise myself I'll research the topic the first chance I get.

"That's so dangerous! Just imagine if it happened to you when you're driving on the highway."

"Yeah, that's why I don't have a driver's license."

I've always found the saying "The devil makes the pots but not the lids" to be misleading; in my experience, lies have the intrinsic quality of creating consistency, causal links, inferences. It's true that I don't have a driver's license, but there's never been a reason for it. Just then, in Sardinia, things fell into place. Not getting a driver's license had been an ethical choice made for myself and for others. Here's my theory: if you simply leave him alone to do his thing, the devil will make both the pots and the lids.

"Ever tried acupuncture?"

Whatever bullshit I come up with in life, there's always someone who asks me that. And in any case, no, I've never tried acupuncture, but I thank them for the advice and write down the name and number of a Chinese doctor who works wonders. I show them my notes to make sure I spelled her name right. If people can believe in miracles, why not believe in narcolepsy, or an inborn imbalance between my femur, tibia, and fibula that for over thirty years kept me from exerting force on bicycle pedals to avoid compromising my spinal column? (I learned to ride a bike at age thirty-five.)

No one has ever called me by my full name, Veronica. My mother claims she wanted to name me Corinna, but then my cousin Corinna was born six months before me, and my aunt stole the name. A typical spat between sisters-in-law. At that point, my mother, unable to choose between Veronica and Erika, officially opted for the former but began using her personal combination, Verika, as soon as I was born.

My father called me Oca—which means "goose" but also "bimbo"—because when I began to talk, in the awkward attempts to pronounce my name I would stammer something like "oooo-ccc-aaa." Oca outlived my childhood to accompany me through adolescence and into adulthood. I was used to it, but always had to explain its origins to people who were astonished or offended when hearing a father calling his own daughter a bimbo. Even as he lay dying, to him I was always Oca. For this reason, whenever I hear a woman called a cow, a vixen, a cougar, a bitch, I'm filled with an absurd feeling of tenderness, and the memory of my father prevails over my indignation.

Most people simply call me Vero, but in addition to Verika, Oca, Scarafona, and Smilzi, I've been: V., Veca, Sveka, Onica, Nicca, Nip, Little Nipple, The Rag, Miss Fringe, and even Hussy. Hussy is what I was called by a guy I met on vacation, with whom one night, during an alcohol-fueled flirtation, I complained about the fact that it sounded great but was unusable as a name. As of the next morning, he decided to redeem, with me, the inauspicious name of Hussy.

Over the last twenty years I've lived in schizoid fashion between Rome and Berlin. Or better, I've lived in Rome while continuing to spend months in Berlin and regretting not living there. There's no real reason for my not moving to Berlin, but if I did move there I'd no longer have a regret that keeps me going day after day. When I'm in Germany, people essentially do call me Veronica, but with a *K*—Veronika— like the rock star I used to dream of becoming. Maybe that's why I can't get myself to move there. How could I ever live up to the name?

In Berlin I don't have a place of my own. Taking advantage of times when friends, or friends of friends, or strangers leave town, I occupy their apartments. From my first escapes from my parents' home to today—when after a long time living with someone I find myself living alone in a studio apartment in Rome—I've stayed in around seventy places. It's no exaggeration. I once took a piece of paper and wrote down a list of them, with all the addresses, like it was a long poem by Ginsberg.

I love living in other people's homes. Discovering their books, their records, their sex toys, the orgasms of their neighbors, using their shampoo, drinking espresso from their cups. That sense of alienation that makes me feel like myself. Unlike the saying about the devil and his pots, I've always taken "Try putting yourself in someone else's shoes" literally. I feel good in other people's shoes, in other people's clothes. I open unfamiliar wardrobes and slip on whatever's there. I look at my reflection in the mirror and recognize myself.

All my books have been written in Berlin in other people's homes. At first the accommodations were more alternative: a squat consisting strictly of gay male vegans who welcomed me despite my being hetero, female, and carnivorous, or the tiny studio of an artist whose walls were painted black and decorated with her works: mechanic's overalls with an axe lodged in them. Then I saw my aging reflected in the bourgeoisification of the homes. I started my last novel in the penthouse of a reporter from Radio Eins, which had a vinyl collection worth fifty thousand euros and an incredibly rare vintage espresso machine. Back then I wore my hair short, and he was the same height as my male relatives. I liked going around wearing his Midwest-folk-singer outfits. One afternoon, his neighbor told me I looked younger without my beard.

I finished the novel in the 130 square meters of the empty apartment of a couple who had just separated. It contained only a bed, a desk, and moving boxes labeled *SHIP TO SARAH*. Sarah had moved to San Francisco. On the desk was a heart-wrenching farewell letter from her and the utility bills to be paid. I wept over the end of a love story before her ex did.

I have problems falling asleep at night.

To try reading a book is counterproductive. If the book's good, I think about how I'll never manage to write one like it, so why should I keep on writing? Why should I keep on doing anything? I might as well stop: stop writing, stop reading, stop smoking, stop existing, just vegetate, go to sleep forever. In fact, that would be the only sensible solution, if only I could fall asleep.

If the book's bad, even the texture of the paper irritates me. My irritation transforms into a deeper thought. I'm moved by the innocent little tree branch sacrificed for such drivel. I feel sorry for all the other innocent little tree branches sacrificed every day for the cause. I think of the bookshops, the libraries, the countless tree-branch cemeteries, the cruel insistence on writing just so we can project an iota of ourselves into the future, can hand down our stories, our memories, to posterity. We're willing to decimate rain forests just to put our words to the press, while that poor posterity—in the scorching heat of the desert, malnourished and prostrate amid mirages of cacti, in their eternal migrations, with their last gasps as they search for a shred of cool respite—will also have to endure our lingering similes, which at the time we thought were as brilliant as comets. And so what keeps me awake is the end of the world.

When I can't fall asleep, I continue to toss and turn in bed, following my own personal choreography. Believing I can't be seen, I give free rein to all the tics I tried to keep bottled up during the day. Then, without fail, there comes an echo to my exasperation.

"Please, Vero, would you stop thumping your heel against the mattress?"

"Could you not keep touching the headboard obsessively?"

"How many more times are you going to crack your elbow?"

In my family, everyone was a big snorer. A full, enveloping sound. It was never quiet at night. It was never quiet in general. There was always something on: the radio, the television, the vacuum cleaner, the hair dryer, the drill, the circular saw. (Saturday was the day my father built walls.) The drywall dividers, chipboard panels, fake doors muffled nothing. We lived immersed in the all-absorbing drone of our bodies and electrical impulses. Compressed and crammed into a home, we were a single organism that wagged its tail, banging it against the partition walls. We talked to each other over the noise, through the noise, which always turned out

to be useful in later claiming the other person had misunderstood you.

Even around the dinner table there was a constant over-
lapping of noises. An uninterrupted murmur that sounded
like an off-key ecclesiastical chant. While other parents
teach their children not to talk with their mouths full, at
my house we went right ahead and ate open-mouthed, which
my mother continues to do today. I've turned what once was
embarrassment into a form of secret enjoyment, leaving the
discomfort to people who are sitting at the table with us and
can't bring themselves to tell a woman in her seventies that
it's not nice to see that clump of cud between her tongue and
palate. My mother even finds it normal to spit stringy bits of
artichoke or meat into her napkin, which she nonchalantly
rolls into a ball and puts on the table. I envy her. I've found
myself sinking into a quiet depression for days simply because someone told me I had a bit of arugula caught between
my teeth. Meanwhile, she can make it through an entire
New Year's Eve feast with that sculpture of bolus beside her
plate. To finish a steak, sometimes she needs more than one
napkin. I remember being at a restaurant where she pulled a
packet of tissues out of her purse to wrap up her confections
of chewed food, which she then tucked into her purse simply
because there wasn't any more room on the table.

The truth is that my mother has always been the real
punk in the family. What could I ever have proved at age

fifteen with my torn fishnet stockings if she was walking
around in a skirt that totally bared her behind? If I tried to
point it out to her, she'd reply, "Why, if it isn't the princess
and the pea!"

The worst thing about that response was that it wasn't
relevant, but at the same time it wasn't entirely irrelevant
either. That is, the story of the princess and the pea didn't
really have much to do with it, but it did have a tiny bit to
do with it, and it was that tiny bit that made me feel like a
nitpicking pain in the ass.

As for my father, he shouted all the time. It was his natural
tone of voice. A person is defined as short-tempered if they
easily lose their temper, but if their temper is permanently
bad, the effect tends to be diminished. It's not like you can
constantly remind a blind person that they can't see. We were
used to it and had stopped noticing it, but if a girlfriend came
over to hang out, she'd always get the feeling she'd stopped
by at a bad time.

"Should I leave? Is Francesca on the phone?"

My father would get home and shout in her face, "So, how's
it going?" which sounded more or less like "What the hell are
you doing in our home?" When she would reply with a terrified "Fine, thanks," the "Glad to hear it!" my father shrieked
back was usually enough to send her fleeing.

Even when he was sleeping, my father resembled one of those snoring bulldogs you see in cartoons.

If I raise my voice, my mother says I got my father's short temper, which he got from my grandpa, who got it from my great-grandpa, whom I never met. I wonder why this genetic defect decided to break its history of descending through the male line by skipping over my brother and landing on me.

As I struggle to fall asleep, tossing and turning in bed, I sense my ancestral temper seething as it keeps all the muscles in my body active. I don't resemble a snoring bulldog. I'm more like a particularly annoying chihuahua.

I've tried natural remedies. Chamomile. Lemon balm. Valerian. Passionflower. Hawthorn. Tasteless swill that smells like rotten grass. Or little tablets I had to take three hours before going to bed. Then two hours before. Then one hour. The last one within just twenty minutes. Well, how was I supposed to know when I'd be going to bed? Nature demanded too much organization.

I turned to meds. The pills people gave me to help me sleep would be slipped into my little pouch of cigarette filters. I became a beggar of spare remedies. It was my way of approaching others, my pickup line. In bathrooms at bars, at concerts, at parties, after watching a play that was proudly sleep-inducing, though unfortunately not enough. Someone was always willing to hand me a pill.

"This will definitely knock you out. You haven't been drinking tonight, have you? If you've been drinking, maybe take just half."

I would drink, then pop two of them.

In the middle of the night I would send them messages saying: "*It didn't work. I'm awake.*" No one ever answered me.

I consulted a doctor. "For how long have you had the impression you haven't been sleeping well?" he asked. Who did he think he was dealing with? I didn't have any impressions. I've always hated people with impressions, sensations, notions. I couldn't sleep, and that was that. He sent me home with a vial of drops whose side effects ranged from paralysis to violent surges in libido.

"Let me know if it works. I'm here if you need me," he said.

I texted the doctor at three a.m. "*Hey, I'm awake!*" Then at four: "*Still awake!*" At five: "*Wide awake!*"

He didn't reply. "*I'm here if you need me.*" *The fuck you are,* I thought. Who knows, maybe he was afraid it was my libido talking.

Sometimes I try masturbating to fall asleep. It's more of a physical exercise, a form of exertion for lazy people who don't care for sports. Or even a mental exercise, a moment of reflection for skeptical people who don't care for meditation.

Men generally fall asleep before me. They might happen to wake up from hearing me fiddling under the covers, and they take it as a provocation. They deliberate what to do, what to succumb to: sex or sleep? At which point I need to explain that it isn't a provocation but the equivalent of a glass of warm milk—intercourse would require too great a dialectical investment, too many variables outside my control, the opposite of what I need—so they can stop deliberating and go back to sleep.

At the height of people stepping up to tell their own experiences with sexual abuse following the #MeToo movement, I remember reading the account of a young woman who'd felt hurt and humiliated because her partner jacked off in bed beside her as she slept. I thought back on all the times I'd found myself in the opposite situation. Had I been insensitive? Had I abused someone without realizing it? And on top of it all, just so I could get a good night's sleep?

However, even that technique ends up failing me. I reach orgasm like the end of a TV series, when all that's left is emptiness and disappointment.

So I try anagramming the names of friends and famous people in my mind, or do diagramless crossword puzzles—rigorously in pen, since I hate pencils. The page gets smeared with ink as I scrawl over words until it all becomes illegible. A bad temper swaddles me like a cashmere blanket. I feel cuddled by the rage of my ancestors.

After peddling any old remedy to me and never answering my late-night texts, the doctor finally, calmly reaches a diagnosis: "Your problem's not insomnia, it's a bad attitude."

My brother became religious of his own accord when he was a child. My mother developed her passion for *fioretti* over the years, and today she goes to mass to spend more time with her son, but when we were little my parents were peacefully agnostic, or at most espoused the Pascalian attitude that, all things considered, you're better off believing. Still, they hadn't even had us baptized, so on Judgment Day they would be saved while we would be left behind wandering in limbo.

In the era before the building of walls, my brother and I slept in a bunk bed, with me below and him above. Before we went to sleep, he would ask, "Are you saying your night-night prayers?"

I don't know if he used the childish term to make his inquisition seem less intimidating. Then he would look down to check whether my hands were clasped. I made sure he saw me concentrating, with my lips reciting an incomprehensible murmur. I'd perfected a sort of *namu myoho renge kyo* with the names of strange little animals. When the night-night prayers were finished, my brother would slide his arm under the railing and dangle it toward me. I would take his hand

and we would fall asleep like that. Saying our prayers was the Viaticum for our good-night ritual, and unless I had my brother's hand to squeeze, I couldn't fall asleep.

Then one day he decided to get baptized. He was in middle school, I was in grade school, and I didn't want to be left behind.

Don Serafino, the priest who was his religious studies teacher, gave him a dozen books so he could read up on the meaning of the sacrament. As for me, he just tossed me a comic book about the life of Jesus. When the day came, during the baptism he asked me a couple questions and I got the answers clamorously wrong. I hadn't even looked at the comic book.

I stood there, mortified, in the little yellow dress bought for the occasion, and didn't know what to say for myself.

Don Serafino stared at me for a long time. "Why do you want to be baptized?"

I drew a blank. I had no idea. Could you flunk a baptism? I searched for my brother's eyes as though for an ask-the-audience lifeline but realized I was on my own. *Never again will you have my hand to hold while you fall asleep,* the look on his face said.

Don Serafino continued to stare at me. At that point I began to get unsettled. In front of me was a priest, but he was also a handsome young man, not even thirty, who was gazing deep into my eyes. I was making things worse for myself before the Lord.

"Are you sure you want to be baptized?" he asked, his voice more caring than angry.

"I dunno."

The solemnity of that "I dunno" must have helped convince him, because he went over to the baptismal font and sprinkled water on my head.

My brother answered all the questions brilliantly and vowed to teach me about the life of Jesus. My mother explained to Don Serafino that I liked to draw.

Despite everything, it was a nice day. After we left the church, my father loaded us into the car and took us out to lunch. I ate Cornish hen, and the memory of that Cornish hen stayed with me for a long time, because days later the Chernobyl nuclear reactor melted down.

In middle school Don Serafino became my teacher too. Every girl in class was in love with him. We were all aquiver when it was time for religious studies. Since it was the same day as physical education, many of us started wearing leggings instead of sweatpants, and the topic ended up being discussed at faculty meetings. Convinced we were doing it to get the attention of the eighth-grade boys, the teachers—all of them female—were concerned that wearing leggings was a slippery slope to letting them feel us up in the washroom. Truth be told, they themselves were sweet on Don Serafino, the only male at school who wasn't a minor. They were always coming up with excuses to knock on his door during religious studies ("Do you have a spare eraser?", "Does anyone know how to unjam the photocopier?") and admire him as he sat, legs spread casually, on the teacher's desk, talking to us about Jesus. With his shirt and clerical collar, Don Serafino never wore those sad worsted wool slacks but a pair of black Teddy Boy jeans. No doubt this topic was being discussed at alternative faculty meetings—the ones the female teachers held at the bar near school.

My entry into middle school was triumphal: thanks to my late baptism, all the other girls in class envied me because Don Serafino's hands had touched my forehead. With growing detail I embellished those exciting minutes by the baptismal font, and thought back on his question "Why do you want to be baptized?" The answer was clearer to me now.

Years later, Don Serafino left the priesthood and got married. I ran into him one day. He was heavyset, with two little kids in tow. His wife looked so old. I must've been around twenty then. It was as if he'd decided to relinquish his vows to go out with one of the teachers rather than one of us. He barely remembered me. I remembered him perfectly well, though I barely recognized him. Without his clergy shirt and Teddy Boy jeans he was any other middle-aged guy taking his family out shopping on Saturday afternoon.

For my brother, faith has its practical side. When he's busy and wants to cut a conversation short, he entrusts me to the Lord.

Let's say I end up calling him with some random question while he's in a meeting at the city hall.

"Somebody asked me to write a porno story. What would you tell them?"

In the background, muffled shouting. Members of the Italian Democratic Party are lodging complaints about the budget.

"You know the parable of the lamp under a bushel?" he asks me.

"No, never heard it. How does it go?"

"Read it."

"I don't have a Bible."

"It's on the internet."

He hangs up.

I google the parable of the lamp under a bushel. I read it but grasp no connection with the porno story. I call my brother back. He's still in the meeting.

"I read it. I don't get it."

"Think it over."

The next day I call him again. Finally I catch him when he's free. "I've thought it over. I still don't get the connection with the story."

"What story?"

S ometimes my brother cheats on God with Freud. He's been in analysis for several years.

I take advantage of his regular sessions to get free therapy. I enjoy having my dreams analyzed. I make them up just to hear them explained. It's like when an advice columnist chooses your letter just because it's clearly fake. I should know, since I've written tons of them.

Lately my brother's been obsessed with the idea that the major repressed memory of my life is an incestuous relationship with nonno Peppino. I've googled this too, but no one has ever bothered to formalize complexes with other family members, so I don't know what name to give mine. After Oedipus and Electra, Peppino sure doesn't sound all that impressive.

Regardless, as a complex, I decide I like it. It's pretty original. And it can't be cured with acupuncture.

Actually, if I had to think of the kind of guy I'm attracted to, the shadow of my grandpa does creep in. Big nose and eyes, prominent forehead, full lips that betray an inherent grimace of smoldering rage. But most of all, the stature.

I distrust tall men. I'm comfortable with the thwarted ambition of scaling one meter seventy. It's easier to embrace them, it's easier to look into their eyes, I can swap clothes with them, and there's no need to readjust their bike seat, now that I know how to ride a bike.

But my brother's theory is even more complex: not only am I in love with my grandpa, but I've also adopted the same model of cohabitation he had with my grandma. They were practically lifelong roommates.

"You have no concept of a couple," he tells me.

"What do you mean by 'couple'?"

But between the two of us, he's the one who's never lived with anyone, except for two former homeless people in their sixties, who've been using his place for around four years now. I lived with someone for over fourteen years, though those who don't know me very well are always visibly surprised to hear it: "Really? I never would've guessed."

I don't know why. Or better, I don't know what the signs of a fourteen-year cohabitation would be, if there's a code, a certain way of talking, of moving, something you can read on a person's face. Maybe it's because I've never managed to use expressions like "my partner," "my boyfriend," "my man," "my lover," "my fiancé." The point is that they've always seemed like ways of showing off, of making a statement, as if to say, "I have one. Do you?" The vibe of an American TV series in which not being asked to prom might jeopardize your entry into society for the rest of your life. Whenever I hear someone say "my wife," "my husband," "my boyfriend," "my partner," I always have the feeling they're trying to prove something, that they want to tell the world they've been asked to prom.

Since I still feel uncomfortable using those expressions, I've always called the person I lived with for fourteen years by his given name, and here I'll call him A.

I can't say whether my brother's theory is right, that I really don't have any concept of a couple, but that's precisely why I know that A. will remain part of my life, because couples—whatever they are—cease to exist, but people don't.

Nonno Peppino and nonna Flora always lived in separate rooms. My grandma's had flowered wallpaper and was full of dressers, nightstands, doilies, and newspaper clippings about religious apparitions or strangers' obituaries. And bourbon bottles, but we would find that out later.

Over the years she grew convinced she was The Chosen One, though it wasn't clear what it was she'd been chosen for. She said God spoke to her. At times He would appear in the sky in the form of a little flame. Other times—more conveniently—He called her on the phone, but when He did she had to put in her hearing aid, because she couldn't hear Him very well. If she wasn't talking to God, she liked chatting on the balcony with the birds and stars.

My grandpa's room was all in 1970s modern antique style, with a radio built into the headboard, the walls white.

The two of them spent their days doing their own thing, and at most they met up over dinner. They didn't even argue about what to watch on television, because she would get dressed up, do up her hair, put on lipstick, make herself comfortable in the living room, and wave at everyone who appeared on the TV screen, while he withdrew to his room and watched TV there in his underwear.

When he was young, my grandpa worked as a shoemaker, but more than instill me with that love straight out of Italian novels for the bygone little world of craftsmen and cobblers, he passed down to me an obsession with shoes. He once had a workshop in Trastevere and lived in a garret above the shop. The problem with poverty is that you never have the foresight to glimpse its romantic potential and make money off it. Grandpa gave up his home and shop to get a job as a worker in a factory—the same one where my father would later become the head of human resources—and with his salary began to pay off the mortgage on an apartment right next to the GRA motorway. Because of this, unfortunately, I never inherited a "*Cozy 1BR apt in Trastevere*" that I could rent out to tourists like the best minds of my generation, but only a cobbler's anvil, which I now use as a doorstop.

*   *   *

When I was little I spent loads of time with nonno Peppino. My folks would leave me with him for weeks, and when they came back to get me I would cling to his leg, whining, as he continued to smoke unperturbed, the cigarette completing the grimace on his face.

One of my deportations to my grandparents' place was made necessary when I began to take my first steps. I tried to move around without anyone noticing, but the second I rose to my feet and tried to toddle on my short legs, my brother would race over and plunk me back down on the floor. Then he would look at my mother and burst out laughing. She also found this hilarious, apparently. So that I wouldn't end up crawling my whole life, they had to do without their favorite game and get me out of there.

Back then, there was nothing around my grandparents' neighborhood. Now there's a dormitory complex and a shopping center. I wish I had a child only so I could take them there and utter the words, "Once this was nothing but countryside."

My grandpa would get dressed up even to go walking in the fields: thick cotton officer's-cut trousers, short-sleeved shirt, and a leather satchel he'd made himself. In the winter he wore a turtleneck and a gray peacoat you might see someone wearing on a bridge crossing the Seine. My brother and I fought over it. Since it fit me better, he's the one who got to keep it. But then again, I already had the anvil. That's how the concept of inheritance works in my family: we take things that embarrass us so we have an excuse for never feeling grown up.

My grandpa would let me sleep in late, then he'd serve me *caffè d'orzo* in an espresso cup to simulate real coffee, and a slice of bread with olive oil and chili pepper. As he waited for my eyes to stop watering he would pop whole peppers into his mouth.

We would go out in the morning to explore and come back in the evening. He scoffed at my father's obsession with hygiene and couldn't wait to let me roll around in the mud and make me eat raw thistles he'd pulled out of the ground. Another of my favorite pastimes was wandering the freshly plowed fields and pretending clumps of earth were cheeses. Without knowing anything about gourmet tastings, I loftily declared various names: "Here we have a Bonfante dei Colli Ottobrini," "Do taste the Portadeux di Verdagnac," "Enjoy the softness of a Corbato di Montefilino." I don't know if I was trying to imitate someone or how I might have come up with a parody of something I knew nothing about, but such marvels, such visionary moments, often emerge in childhood. I reserved mine for cheeses.

I loved country life, and my dream was to have a farm, which conflicted with my other dream of becoming a world-famous rock star. Then it occurred to me that one day Veronika could retire from the stage and spend the rest of her life surrounded by pigs and chickens, reading all the fan mail people continued to send her.

When we went out for a walk, my grandpa always had his thirty-five-millimeter camera around his neck in a leather case, it too handcrafted. If there are any photos of me from my childhood, it's thanks to him, but since he couldn't stand my shyness in front of the lens, he would tell me to turn around, in the middle of a plowed field, by a sheep pen, or on an overpass. So I would turn around and stand there.

"What do I do?"

The artist would refuse to answer me.

When we went to pick up the pictures, we'd find ourselves with a chic fashion shoot, the edge of the city in the background, an acid mix of rural life and postindustrial architecture. It's just that instead of a pouting model there was a little figure seen from behind who wore shorts, her arms dangling.

When I was little, only on rare occasions did they dress me as a girl. Hand-me-downs made the whole round of all the older cousins before being given to my brother and then finally to me. I also always wore my hair short, because of a purely adult concept of practicality. "It makes things easier at the pool," my parents claimed. It's a shame they never signed me up for swimming lessons.

When using public restrooms, I often ended up being glared at by some mother who thought she'd just caught a young sex maniac sneaking into the ladies' room.

Once, while I was going really high on the swings, next to me was an awkward little girl who couldn't get started swinging on her own. When I stared at her triumphantly from my unreachable heights, she burst out crying. Her mother decided to give the girl her first lesson in feminism: "Never you mind what the boys do."

At night my grandpa and I would get into bed together, both in our undershirts and underwear. Once I entered puberty my parents began to wonder whether it was a bad idea, us being under the sheets like that together.

"Keep Scarafona at home with you, then," was my grandpa's reaction.

Moving into my grandma's room would've been absurd. The two of us were practically strangers. We waited our turn for the bathroom and after dinner each of us washed our own dishes. Then she'd put on some lipstick and spend the evening looking pretty for Pippo Baudo, on the TV screen.

And so I kept on sleeping in my grandpa's bed, until it got embarrassing even for me. I remember the first Sunday I left his place just to avoid spending the night. My grandpa didn't even get up from his armchair. I could tell he was bothered by the platitudes, the excuses, my initiation into duplicity. My grandma waved goodbye from the balcony, then went back to chatting with the stars.

On the bus back I felt heroic and really bummed. I'd made one of the first deliberate choices of my life, but I'd been dishonest, and modesty had turned into distance. I would never learn to eat a chili pepper without crying.

Shortly after that, my grandma grew ill. She had a gown made for herself, a sky-blue angel gown complete with wings, so she could more easily fly away once she was dead. She often wrote to the Pope, and though the Holy Father didn't reply to all her letters, he would nevertheless send her best wishes for a happy Easter and a merry Christmas. Near the end, she made the effort to write and reassure him that she would rise again. "For the time being, though, Your Holiness can hold off on the greeting cards."

She was taken to the hospital, and my grandpa never went to visit her. "I already said goodbye to her," he told my father, who insisted on taking him there.

When my grandma died, he didn't even want to see how pretty she was, dressed as an angel in the casket, with a new hearing aid bought just for the occasion, and he stopped going out on his walks. He stayed barricaded inside his place, in his armchair. My cousin took a black-and-white snapshot of him in that armchair. In the picture, the grimace on his face is different from his usual one, though there's no remorse to it, only exhaustion.

"I said goodbye to her," he kept saying. Then he stopped talking altogether. He grew ill too. Died just a few months later. During the days of the G8 summit in Genoa.

"Thank God your grandfather's dying," my mother told me and my brother. That is, thank God we wouldn't be joining the protests in Genoa.

When we remind her about it, she doesn't deny it, but she can't see why it's strange. The only moral principle she recognizes is her own anxiety.

When my father grew ill, many years after the G8 in Genoa, deep down I made the same decision my grandpa had. He was in the hospital. I went there every day, usually in the afternoon. He was always lucid, but tired easily. Actually, I think he would pretend to sleep because he didn't feel like hearing words anymore. One time I was telling him about an essay I had just translated. There wasn't anything particularly interesting about the essay, a pretentious, unnecessarily complicated American work, but I was forcing myself to find some topic of conversation, like everyone did, because that was how it worked. He was nodding, his eyes closed.

Then I realized I'd already said to him all the things I would ever want to say to him in my lifetime. There wouldn't be others. He'd be gone. So I said goodbye to him. I got up from my chair to leave.

"Papà, I'm saying goodbye," I told him.

He nodded again.

"Papà . . . I'm *really* saying goodbye."

"Yeah, yeah."

"Papà, do you understand?"

Silence.

"Hey, Papà, I'm—"

"All right already, he heard you," snapped the man in the next bed.

I don't know if he understood, if he forgave me, given that he hadn't forgiven his own father.

When I came back in the days after that, I stopped making an effort. I put up with the silence like someone puts up with boredom in a waiting room. I brought a book to read or translated my pretentious, unnecessarily complicated essays for under ten euros a page.

Sometimes he asked me if I needed money. I said no, even if it wasn't true.

I made sure he was hydrated, moved his legs so they wouldn't swell, and asked the man in the next bed if he needed anything. Every gesture was mechanical. There was no devotion or filial affection. Rather, it was a way to occupy space, to trust in actions, a human instinct toward a body that was suffering.

I didn't want to have memories of that body.

For me, my father was gone.

But the bodies of the ill change other bodies. I'd seen A. shave my father, smooth back the delicate layer of skin left on his cheeks, take care of his catheter. I'd watched him with a sense of gratitude that ended up contaminating other glimpses.

Right after the funeral I left for Berlin. My bed in Rome had become an unlivable place, the theater of an unwholesome orgy. There were traces of my worst nights, A. and I always tired, fragile, him asleep and me wide awake; there were the outlines of his parents, who'd come to visit my father, of my mother, who'd spent the night there a few times after we ate pizza together near the hospital. I don't know why it is that at the most dramatic moments of my life I always end up eating pizza.

I stayed in Berlin for three months in an apartment that had a single room with lots of light, a bathroom down the hall, and a shower set up inside the closet. I squeezed into that closet and stayed there for hours, the stifling space reminding me of my childhood. I spent my days alone, slept alone, but hungered for bodies; they'd become both pure abstraction and pure matter—I contemplated them from a distance, obsessive, restless, overcome by maniacal voyeurism. I stared at boys' arms, hands, at all men's gestures that didn't make me think of patient care. Anything would do: elbows resting on a counter, a shoulder pushing open a door, fingers zipping up a windbreaker. Across the street from the apartment was a park. I would wait for groups of high schoolers to swarm into it when class got out; through the window I'd watch them shooting hoops or holding a ping-pong tournament. My favorites were two punks who were chess fanatics. They would stay until nightfall, moving the pieces around with hands clad in fingerless woolen gloves. On the street, I would fixate on waiters tucking money into the leather pouches around their waists, workers assembling scaffolding at a construction site and opening bottles of beer with their lighters. I was happy there was always construction work going on in Berlin. I would stop to watch someone unlocking their bike from a post and inflating the tires, or unwrapping a pack of cigarettes; I ached at the sight of a hand slipped into the jeans of a girl walking in front of me. I was incapable of longing, if not in that form. I feared contact, the obscenity of contact, and yet I would closely watch even the briefest of touches, like I had when I was little, when I spied on the kids kicking around a toad. Might the truth have been that I'd wished I could take a kick at it too but would never have admitted it? But then again, I wouldn't be able to admit it even now.

My mother called me ten times a day to remind me of her loneliness. Her husband had just died and her daughter had abandoned her. "What are you doing in Berlin, anyway?" she would ask. Nothing, as always. I was watching men.

When I got back to Rome I found A.'s body again. Fortunately it had returned to being his body.

Only once did I go to visit my father at the cemetery. It was awful, especially aesthetically. He's buried at Prima Porta. I challenge any graveyard poet to wander within its cement walls and find inspiration for an elegy.

There's also a bigger reason than my romanticism for why I don't go to visit my father, which is that I'm lazy. Prima Porta is on the very edge of town, outside the GRA. Since I don't have a driver's license, it would take me a good hour to get there using public transportation. And once there, it would take me another hour to find his tomb, because I can't read the maps. I've never bothered to check if he has fresh flowers in his vase, or how much dust has settled on his photograph.

My brother has them hold a memorial mass every year to commemorate his death. It often turns out I'm not in Rome that day, because the date falls during the Berlinale. I usually wake up that morning, still hungover from some awful party the night before, to find a text from my mother on the phone: "*There's always someone looking down on you from heaven.*"

It should be a sweet message reminding me that my father is watching over me even in the afterlife, but my guilt over forgetting yet again the commemoration of his death makes me read it like a mob boss's coded message, somewhere between the threatening and the dystopian. Sometimes my mother makes an effort and comes up with something that fits the theme: "*Even in the skies over Berlin you'll find your father's angel.*"

I stay in bed a moment longer, thinking about how to reply, as my father's watchful gaze clears up my hangover. I'm lucid and sad.

My mother waits, then can't resist. She wants at least a bit of satisfaction from me. *"Did you catch the movie reference?"*

When I leave the apartment, the skies over Berlin fill with shadows. The awkward feeling lingers all day thanks to the messages my mother continues to send me as I'm sitting in the movie theater.

"We're here with Christian and your aunt. You're the only one missing!", "A big hug from your mother, your big brother and your father!", "We even said a little prayer for our family's little girl!", "It's important to stay close to one another!", "Remember that your father will never abandon you!", "Mamma and Papà will be with you forever!"

I long for the day to be over as soon as possible, turn down invitations to parties being thrown by Armenian and Belorussian directors, but the messages hound me until late that night.

"Did you miss your Papà today?", "Are you sad there, all alone?", "Could you feel our big, big hug?"

I still have my father's clothes: jackets and shirts, a watch. The shoes are a bit big on me, even though we had the same size feet, because since he was ashamed of how small his were, he bought shoes one size bigger. I also kept one of the photos of him that I like. It's of him on a business trip to Germany, his hand stretched out in front of his face in a typical expression of his, when he would seem to be saying, "Well, take a look at you!"

Beside him is a colleague whose name I can't remember. Actually, the guy's taking up even more space than my father, because he towers at least twenty centimeters above him. He's in profile, smoking.

I put the picture in a frame and always keep it on my desk. I would've felt bad cutting out his colleague, so he stayed in. When someone notices the picture on my desk and asks who the two are, I answer, "The short one's my father."

"And the other one?"

It occurs to me that keeping a picture more than half of which is filled with some tall guy whose name I don't even know reflects my notion of mourning.

M y paternal grandparents are buried in a little town in the province of Teramo. I don't go there either. Once in a while my mother makes a point of reminding me that she's still the one who pays the electricity bill my father used to pay, to keep alive her in-laws' cemetery light.

"I do it gladly," she tells me.

"Okay."

"I'm happy to do it."

"Good."

"Of course, your aunt has never wondered who pays the bill now, but it's no problem."

"No, of course not."

"Want to know how much it costs me every year?"

That's her way of honoring the dead: paying the electricity bill for her in-laws and her husband, as well as for her mother, who's buried in the cemetery of a horrible little village in the hinterland of Foggia, in Puglia. That cemetery is the only one I've ever gone to regularly.

My mother's mother, nonna Muccia, made us go there whenever we went to stay with her. We had to visit the whole round of dead relatives dating back to the 1800s: honor killings described with a touch of pride, illnesses that had ancient names—gout, pellagra, the scourge of the Spanish influenza—men who keeled over from sunstroke in the fields, women done in from childbirth or beatings, babies that were stillborn. At each grave we left a flower and kissed the photograph. The inscriptions on the tombstones always contained a few typos. My brother and I would compete to see who could find more of them. Then my grandmother would make us stand for ten minutes staring at the photo of her late husband. She just had to remind us that he resembled movie star Amedeo Nazzari, and then she would burst into tears. At that point my mother wept too, my brother said a prayer, my father disinfected with alcohol the vase holding the flowers, and I stood there waiting for the ten minutes to be over.

I never loved nonna Muccia and, happily, the feeling was mutual.

My brother was her favorite grandchild. That's not my interpretation—she used to say it repeatedly to the whole host of us cousins gathered together on holidays. As for me, what was she supposed to do with a skinny, quiet, depressed little girl who took no interest in her grandmother's cooking? She'd been a widow for years, since before I was born, but she clung to her mourning with the tenacity of a die-hard soccer fan. She reserved for all other widows the scorn diehards felt for bandwagon fans.

"That one there only dresses in black because it's slimming."

She lived in a three-story house that still today sets the stage for my nightmares. When we went to visit her she would greet us at the front door, ruddy-faced and covered with flour, her wavy hairdo fresh from the salon and stinking of hair spray and air freshener.

While my father unloaded the suitcases and my mother rubbed her temples because, as always, she'd gotten a migraine from arguing in the car, nonna Muccia would smother my brother in a big hug for ten minutes, but with me she just squished her massive boobs in my face once, quickly, as though to stake her claim.

Not only was I a skinny little girl with no appetite, but I was growing into an adolescent who was shamelessly flat-chested. My grandmother was always eager to repeat the mantra she'd learned from her late husband: "You've got to fill at least a champagne glass."

With this, she would slap an espresso cup against my chest and burst out laughing.

Summer after summer, the fun and surprises never ended. If company was over, she would pull the cup away from my chest and do it all over again with unwavering zeal: "Not even an espresso cup."

This was followed by other laughs, jeers, reassurances, motivational talks directed at my tits, and then the cup was placed back on the dish rack.

As long as she lived, I never gave my grandmother the satisfaction of filling that cup. But she can rest in peace: after her death, nothing changed. The first time I was offered champagne in the special coupe, I couldn't help but visualize the folds of her aged tits overflowing the edge of the glass.

I'm the only woman in my family—on both the maternal and paternal sides—who doesn't have tits. Despite this—or probably because of this, following that solid principle of domestic hazing which gloriously keeps family hierarchies alive—for my birthday I was inevitably given the gift of a bra.

Since I had no use for one, its size was completely arbitrary. I have a dresser drawer full of immaculate bras, the tags still on them, ranging from extra small to extra large, in lace, in satin, with underwire, padded, with and without straps.

I can't get rid of them, partly because presents are sacred to me and I'm always afraid karma will retaliate, partly because the perversion of that drawer reminds me of the intrinsic moral truth of a family.

As a matter of fact, I have a drawer that's even more up-setting. It's full of the little newborn-baby outfits my mother buys for my future offspring, even though she knows I don't want kids.

"I'm not doing it for you," she tells me. "I'm doing it for my grandchildren."

On the other hand, the trousseau my grandmother set aside for me for when I get married (another unfulfilled wish, along with my filling a champagne glass) and against which my mother proudly rebelled ("My daughter's going to choose whatever linens she wants!") ended up in my moth-er's hands, so while she sleeps in fancy sheets embroidered with my initials, I wallow in an unclaimed freedom made of Ikea cotton.

My mother treats her filial love as an achievement, as an escape from blind, desperate brutality. My grandmother tried to abort her by jabbing a hanger into her uterus. The family stories contain no other details about the event, just the ob-vious fact that something definitely went wrong, given that my mother was born.

I've always wanted to know more, not only because her failed abortion is directly connected to my very existence, but also because I'd like to be able to draw a connection from a seventeen-year-old girl who already had two kids and was willing to stab herself with a hanger to a cheerful old woman who liked to squish her boobs in my face. I wonder if in the omitted details of that connection, my grandmother and I might ever have managed to find ourselves feeling mutual affection.

It never happened.

The summers my brother and I spent in Puglia helped perfect our devotion to boredom, but unlike me, he was interested in nonna Muccia's cooking, so he betrayed me with a burst of enthusiasm when she let him dip a piece of bread into the ragù that had been simmering over a low flame for hours.

Like all Pugliesi, my grandmother was convinced her *pagnotte* were the best in the world. They had such dense, heavy crumb and such limp crust that when you pulled out the bread sopping with sauce it looked like you'd fished out a kitchen sponge that had fallen into the pot.

Since I didn't eat (one of the reasons blamed for my lack of boobs), at nonna Muccia's I spent all day in the guest room on the ground floor, which was the coolest floor in the house, and could dedicate myself to boredom without pointless distractions. The problem was that by staying on the ground floor, I also became the person in charge of welcoming anyone who happened to ring the doorbell. I would go answer it and generally found myself staring at a puzzled face.

"Oh, are you Gianna's daughter?"

"No."

"Titina's daughter?"

"No."

"Pasqualino's new *zita*?"

"No."

Every time I opened the door I had to explain my parental relation, which turned out to be the only time I ever opened my mouth all summer during my stay at the house.

"Oh, you're Franca's daughter! How'd you grow so tall without becoming a woman yet?"

One day, at the door I found zio Uccio. I don't even know if he was actually my uncle, but I called him *zio*, like all the grown-up men who stopped by. Zio Uccio was shorter than me and about three times as wide. He was bald, except for a greasy comb-over that started at his forehead and branched out over his skull like a dried-up estuary.

"You got a comb?" he asked me.

I took my uncle over to the ground-floor bathroom. He walked into the bathroom behind me and closed the door.

"So you're Franca's daughter?"

"Yes."

He stared at me as though it were the beginning of a great philosophical dialogue. "So, want to comb your uncle's hair?"

With this, he pulled his dick out of his pants, making it difficult for me to find any connection with his comb-over, which led to a moment of hesitation before I dumped the comb on the floor and raced out of the bathroom, because

I was a girl who valued logic. He muttered a few curses—all unintelligible to me, partly because they were in dialect, partly because he was keeping his voice low, given that his wife was upstairs—then went up without even touching his hair.

I never told anyone about zio Uccio's dick.

It had nothing to do with shame or repressed memories, not at all. Actually I was pleased it happened; it gave me the perfect excuse to continue to silently detest that house and my summers in Puglia, the smell of sauce, the soggy bread, the *orecchiette, cavatelli, nevole, scarcelle, grano dei morti, taralli, lampascioni, torcinelli*, and the hard-boiled egg cooked inside the roasts.

When all things Apulian became the rage—Salento, the *pizzica*, the revival of *tarantolati*, the rediscovery of Ernesto De Martino—when intellectuals were restructuring trulli and Vendola seemed to be the savior of the homeland, I clung to my memories. Family dinners with the womenfolk who cooked the food, served the meals, and washed the dishes while the menfolk stayed sprawled in their armchairs, snoring (I was excused from both activities: my short hair and flat chest made me a creature good for nothing beyond combing uncles' hair); the *controra,* when it was too stifling to breathe but you couldn't leave the house; the Romanian caregivers bullied by day and fucked as soon as the old women fell asleep; the trips to the seaside, driving through the scorching

heat of the Apulian plains with boiling-hot baking pans of
lasagna on your lap and five kids squeezed into the back seat.

During one of those trips (zio Carmine behind the wheel),
suddenly on the deserted road there appeared a young
woman covered with blood.

"Speed up," was my aunt's reaction.

All five of us children were glued to the window.

My uncle pulled over, cursing. The girl dragged herself
toward us, her top in tatters. One of her breasts was bared.

My aunt didn't take it well. "The tramp!"

Nevertheless, zio Carmine got out of the car.

They'd had an accident, driven off the side of the road. At
the bottom of the ravine were three young people in agony.
She'd managed to climb back up. We were the first human
beings to pass by. Our car door was locked, but my brother
and I climbed over the seat into the front. My aunt held us
back by our waistbands, hysterical, then let go.

"Don't you dare," she warned her children.

The air was torrid and the sun blazing. Mirages on the
asphalt shimmered to the horizon beneath the cloudless sky,
that infinite blue of the South that today makes me think of
death.

My brother and I looked over the edge at the overturned
car and the three bodies scattered among the dry weeds and
wreckage. From the ravine came inarticulate groans that
didn't even sound human, like the cries of cats in heat.

"The littl'un is thirsty," my uncle told the girl with a huge shrug of his shoulders, jutting his chin toward my baby cousin, whose face was still pressed against the window. The girl stared at him, not understanding.

He ordered me and my brother back into the car. The girl began to plead with him.

"The littl'un is thirsty," he repeated. This time, not even a shrug.

My brother and I stood there, stock-still, until my uncle whacked us both across the face to get us back into the car.

"All the whuppings your mother never gave you," my aunt muttered.

I couldn't stop crying. My baby cousin sank into a mire of embarrassment. Our elder cousins looked us in the eye with the fatalism of two eighty-year-olds. My uncle started up the car and left behind the girl and the bodies lying in the sun.

Zio Uccio's dick wasn't the first one I'd ever seen. In a way, I was already prepared for the fact that there were men who wanted to show me theirs, though it was unclear to me why.

During my first year in middle school, my brother would walk me there and then continue on to his high school. It was a hard-won privilege, freeing myself from my mother's perpetually late VW Bug and my father's perpetually early Opel Kadett. For months they'd dropped me off in front of the school either half an hour before or half an hour after the school bell rang. Then, toward spring, my parents allowed me to go there on my own with my brother. He was probably less enthusiastic about this big development than me, and he avenged himself by spending the time talking about Jesus or about Matteotti. (He'd gotten into politics.)

One morning in April, as he was explaining the reasons for the schism between the Catholic and Orthodox Churches, we ran into Isabella, a classmate of his to whom he dedicated quatrains ("*Your eyes of hazel brown / Your purple button-down . . .*"), which theoretically I shouldn't have read and therefore had read very avidly, along with all his unsent love letters, seasoned with tender masturbatory dreams.

Isabella actually did have eyes that were light brown and deep, like "*Nutella in the jar / Lit up by a star.*" Her skin looked tan even in winter, and her blond hair was tied up in a perfect little ponytail that marked time like a metronome. She often wore button-downs, though they weren't purple and didn't rhyme with the color of her eyes. In any case, the sight of Isabella on our way to school threatened my brother's moral fiber.

What to do? Could he really ditch his little sister? Leave her oblivious to the fundamental reasons for the Great Schism?

Isabella, perhaps not completely unaware of his suffering, simply flashed him a look with her hazel eyes. My brother scratched a few whiskers of his nonexistent beard, a gesture that still today reveals his agitation when he's grappling with a biblical dilemma and is afraid of succumbing to evil.

He looked at me, hoping for some sign of consent to leave me behind. For a moment I kept him on tenterhooks, putting on the expression of a terrified little girl, then I winked at him: I had just learned how to and still got a kick out of doing it.

And so he gave me a peck on the cheek, a few warnings, and abandoned me for the last fifty meters separating me from the school gates. As he walked off with Isabella, I stared blankly at the perfect ponytail that represented both fraternal betrayal and my freedom.

It was the first time I'd ever been on the street alone. The asphalt was covered with fluff from the poplar trees like a giant bubble bath. I imagined it as the stage for one of Veronika's concerts, the spotlights shining down from above, and her, slowly emerging from the whiteness.

After not even ten steps, I heard someone whisper, "Pssst, pssst."

I looked around.

Again, "Pssst, pssst."

I repeated the sound, like it was a songbird's call.

At that point, a guy popped out from behind a car and opened his raincoat. At the time I knew nothing about the existence of flashers, not to mention that they actually wore a regulation uniform: a raincoat with nothing beneath it.

All I managed to see was a shapeless, reddish protuberance. A mass. It lasted seconds. Then the guy closed his raincoat and disappeared.

And so, for a long time, I imagined that a dick was shaped more or less like a spongy, lumpy nose. Now I knew why they usually kept it hidden in their underwear. But then why had that man wanted to show me his? Maybe it was to give me a glimpse of some unspeakable truth: look at the burden we have to bear!

That mass hounded me over the next few days. In my mind it grew huge, deformed. A nebula of flesh in constant expansion. At home I couldn't bear to look at my brother or father. It seemed unbelievable that they were keeping that galaxy of organic matter hidden in their pants, incredible that they lived with it day after day.

I was struck by a doubt: what if the man in the raincoat had been trying to tell me he was sick? What if it was a cry for help? Otherwise, why on earth would he have shown it to me?

There was no way for me to make a comparison—what was a dick shaped like, a healthy dick, that is?—nor did I know who to ask. I searched my brother's notebooks for answers, but not even his odes to Isabella turned out to be helpful. His poetic transfigurations made what I was looking for unintelligible. "*Between my legs a rock / When I see you on my block.*"

What a strange picture, I thought.

The night came when I couldn't resist anymore. "I think I saw a rock," I blurted out at dinner.

"What do you mean?"

I explained what I meant.

My parents were furious with my brother, and the next morning my mother took me not just to school but all the way to my classroom. She went up to the Italian teacher and explained to her why she was there.

"The girl believes she's seen a wiener," she said.

Unfortunately Massimo Carocci, in the front row, over-heard her, and within minutes the whole class had been in-formed that *the girl believed she'd seen a wiener.*

All morning long kids passed me drawings of dicks, charming miniatures that looked nothing at all like my vi-sion of the reddish protuberance, which turned out to be almost reassuring. Then came a series of gallant invitations to peek beneath the desks while the boys waggled a hand in their pants to simulate—I think—an erection.

The story of the wiener went on for a few days, until, luckily, it was obscured by the courageous feats of Mimmo Tenaglia—repeat student of class 3B and school sex symbol just one notch below Don Serafino—who in the girls' bath-room had placed his in Stefania Chirianni's hand.

The threat of the reddish mass lost its vigor, gently sagged: if that thingy could be held in a girl's hand, I told myself, it couldn't be so scary. Seeing zio Uccio's dick made me certain of it.

After that, encounters with flashers became a classic during my childhood. My neighborhood was well suited to accommodate them: there were lots of trees and bushes, few streetlights, and long porticoes to pop out from. Even the bus going downtown, with its hot crush of bodies, was a place where perverts never felt unwelcome. At age twenty, on a crowded tram coming back from the university with Cecilia, suddenly I felt something squishy and damp in my hand that I couldn't identify. I thought it was a dog's tongue. Cecilia cleared things up for me.

"You think I should scream?" I asked her.

"Meh, your call."

I turned to its owner simply to inform him where his dick had ended up and to invite him to take it back.

Last summer, at the beach, as I was sitting on some rocks at the water's edge, smoking while I waited for a girlfriend to come back from a swim, a guy came up behind me and asked for a cigarette. I turned around and found myself facing a twentysomething guy with his swimsuit in his hand and a solid boner.

Whenever I'm asked for a cigarette, I feel obligated to offer one. As a principle, I always do. I hate people who come up with excuses not to. The same goes for people who don't pass the joint and pretend they forgot. So I handed him my tobacco pouch and asked him to put his swimsuit back on.

Instead, he just sat down beside me and started rolling. We stayed there facing the sea with our cigarettes. I didn't know what to do: I couldn't go into the water, because I didn't know how to swim. And I couldn't climb down from the rocks because I would've had to climb over his naked body, boner and all. My girlfriend's head was a distant speck on the horizon. Then I thought of calling my brother. I put him on speaker and asked how his job as culture councillor was going. It worked. After less than five minutes of cultural politics in the northeast outskirts of Rome, the guy went limp.

Sometimes, though, cultural politics in the northeast outskirts of Rome can have the opposite effect. When my brother fights against the removal of a Roma camp or a migrants' squat, for example, his Facebook wall sees a surge of eroticism. There are men who wish upon my mother and me numerous sexual relations with a whole host of Romanians or Africans (from which African country, they don't specify). In general these are nonconsensual relationships that entail anal penetration, though in some cases they grant us the privilege of intentionally deriving pleasure from it. One time my mother called me gripped with her usual anxiety, but she was rather curious too. "Verika: would you explain all this talk about a 'gang bang'?"

Summer has always been problematic for me, even when I wasn't being deported to the dark heart of Puglia.

In fifth grade, just before final exams, I came down with rheumatic fever, to general jubilation in my family of hypochondriacs at the discovery that one of us had an actual illness.

It was a sweltering June and I was bedridden, my joints stiff and my legs covered with a reddish rash. I couldn't even make it to the bathroom without someone carrying me there. It wasn't a really serious illness, but it wasn't pretty.

My father came up with mental associations, like *rheumatism = no humidity*. For starters, he decided I shouldn't bathe, so he just disinfected me with rubbing alcohol from head to toe. My skin became scaly. Then he decided I shouldn't sweat. The internet wasn't around back then, so there was no way for me to verify whether what my father was saying was bullshit. If he got it into his head that I couldn't sweat, then I—lying there, perfectly still—tried my very best not to.

"Read a book, though," my mother told me.

My family of well-read hypochondriacs couldn't come to terms with the fact that in fifth grade all I read was Mickey

Mouse comics or, at most, the abridged version of *Little Women*. But still, I didn't want to be Jo. I didn't want to be any of them. I hated the entire March female family line and harbored the secret desire they would all meet with a terrible fate.

My brother decided to sacrifice himself for the cause. He sat down on the edge of my bed to read me *Animal Farm*. I passionately followed the intrigues of the terrible pigs, while he delved into the allegorical subtext. He explained the history of Communism, of the USSR, all the way to perestroika. He told me perestroika was the splotch on Gorbachev's forehead. I believed it until seventh grade, when I wrote it in a paper that was sadistically read aloud by the Italian teacher.

Meanwhile, my classmates in fifth grade took their final exams and left on summer vacation. My great love at the time, Stefano Bellucci, came over with his mother to see me.

My father had had a brilliant idea: wrapping a roll of paper towels around my body to protect me from sweat. Stefano Bellucci and his mother stared at the spongy bulges beneath my cotton undershirt and said nothing. Neither of them had the courage to ask what I was doing bundled in paper towels. That was the end of our great love.

I quickly forgot him. In the days spent in bed with the new torment of *The Brothers Karamazov* read aloud by my brother, the only moments I had to look forward to were visits from the doctor.

The physician looking after me was called Dr. Del Bosco. He was a rather tall man who always had to stay slightly hunched over in our apartment, to avoid banging his head against the tunnel of storage space. He was a little younger than my parents and had huge green eyes full of speckles, like a cartoon character's, and gorgeous, slender hands.

While 1800s Russia faded into the background amid my brother's yawns, I did nothing but think of those hands, obsessively imagining them on me until they actually were on me. Dr. Del Bosco's hands lifting my undershirt, unrolling the layers of paper towels, tapping me on the back as he listened to my chest with a stethoscope, rubbing lotion on my rash-covered legs. And then his voice, warm but authoritative: "Now roll over." And again his hands on my back. "Breathe in." The stethoscope gliding down my spine. He lowered my shirt. Wadded the paper towels into a ball. Smiled at me complicitly, as if to say, "What can you do? Your father's crazy."

When the doctor walked out of my room, bending over to make it through the folding door, I overheard his conversation in the hallway with my parents.

"A quick sponge bath wouldn't hurt . . ."

"Well, we'll see," my father replied.

"Well, we'll see," was his nice way of saying "Forget it," which I'd learned the hard way in my useless attempts to

persuade him to give me a bicycle or roller skates. My mother
had it worse, because she was trying to persuade him to give
her another child.

Even without the rheumatic fever, in my family bathing has
always been a bit strange. The walls dissecting our house had
reached the bathroom, leaving no room for the bidet, but
then again none of us had ever used it. Showers were taken
only on Sundays. The rest of the time, a good rubdown with
alcohol was enough. My father always took rubbing alcohol
and paper towels with him wherever he went. He disinfected
café tables, silverware, water bottles, supermarket shelves,
packets of cigarettes, door handles in shops, keypads on ATM
machines and on public telephones, and naturally phone
receivers (even at friends' homes). Wherever we went on
vacation we spent the first day cleaning every last surface
with alcohol and lining the drawers with paper towels. Still,
the idea of improving our personal hygiene was never taken
into consideration.

Years after my grandma and grandpa died, my father started building walls in their home too, turning
a seventy-square-meter apartment into two cozy little
microapartments.

Today their place is up for sale, and the real estate agent
trying to sell it sends me feedback from the people who've

gone to see it, listing its strengths and weaknesses. Most people are simply bewildered when they walk through the front door and find themselves staring at two doors and two apartments instead of one, but what always tops the "Weaknesses" list is: "*There's no bidet.*"

Before fully reaching puberty, when people at school started pointing out that I smelled funny, I'd always imagined one shower a week was the socially accepted universal standard. As soon as I insisted on showering every day, my mother took it as a provocation. She would open the bathroom door on me. "Get your hands off yourself."

Privacy was a concept my mother always fought hard against. It's no wonder that at our place there wasn't a single door that could be locked. When my brother and I talked on the phone, she would stand there right behind us, suggesting answers, a habit she hasn't lost over the years, and still today if we happen to get a call on our cell phones in her presence, especially if it's a work call, she's more than happy to chip in her two cents.

"Ask how much they're going to pay you."

"Come on, please, go away."

"Fine, but how much are they going to pay you?"

"No, sorry, I wasn't talking to you . . ."

"Hand me the phone. I'll ask them."

Since I'm still listed as a resident at my mother's address (my laziness is more persistent than any possible desire for liberation), if any mail for me shows up there, she calls me, all excited.

"There's a letter from Mondadori publishers. Should I open it?"

"No thanks, Mamma. There's no need."

"What if it's money?"

"I doubt Mondadori is going to send me cash in an envelope."

"Well, listen. The letter says that . . ."

Getting back to Dr. Del Bosco, I was irrevocably in love with him. I could think of nothing else. He brought me ice cream every time he came over, and secretly washed my chest and underarms using a basin he got from the bathroom. He told my parents he needed it to dilute some lotion. What would drive him to lie for me if not love?

I convinced myself that my feelings were reciprocated, and the conviction grew stronger when my parents mentioned he was separating from his wife.

The final confirmation came when he moved into a rented apartment in my building. I could hear our hearts beating across the seven flights of stairs, the whispers—"Roll over . . . breathe in . . ."—and two desperate souls finally meeting halfway, on the fourth-floor landing. For the moment I was just a smelly girl with stringy hair who was all bundled up in paper towels, but soon I would be better again and would run to him.

I had a nagging doubt, though: What if my illness was the reason for our love? Would he take care of a girl who was healthy?

Months later, the first time I left the house, still abstaining from showers, I ran into him outside the front door of our building. He wasn't alone. He greeted me warmly and introduced me to Laura. I glowered at her. Yeah, he'd left his wife for someone younger, but not *that* much younger.

During my convalescence, Dr. Del Bosco would stop by from time to time to check on me, but I became withdrawn and tried to keep my mind off his hands. Meanwhile, he entrusted me to the care of a nurse who would give me a penicillin shot twice a week. The nurse's name was Fausto. He was from Viterbo and wielded his accent with a touch of pride. He was one of those men who think that in order to be brilliant you need a tried and tested repertoire of jokes. Actually, he specialized in what's-the-worst jokes. Since our house was full of books, he tried to work them into his act.

"You know what's the worst for a dictionary?"

"No."

"Not having the last word."

"Oh."

Fausto called me "Little Miss Bigmouth" because I didn't like to chat and never laughed at his worsts. There was more resentment than affection in the nickname, but nothing could make him give up on his worsts.

Since penicillin was quite dense, the needle was thick and the injection painful. Fausto would start by giving me a slap on the ass, then another, then yet another, then finally there came the pinch of the injection. The first couple tries often failed. Fausto would laugh and blame it on my "tough hide." At that point, he would resort to a distraction.

"What's the worst for a scaredy-cat editor?"

"That hurt."

"Having to work with a ghostwriter."

The entire operation was accompanied by his sound effects to make the experience more complete: *whap, ka-poom, plink, plonk, zap.* I don't know why my mother with her sexophobia didn't deign to intervene in his onomatopoeic spankings.

F or three years after that I continued to live with a dread of sweating. I don't know how my father came up with the notion of three years, but he did. He'd check my back and armpits: if there was any trace of dampness, he would panic and come back armed with a roll of paper towels. I spent our summers at the seaside beneath a beach umbrella with a T-shirt on and paper towels wrapped around my body. If some fearless boy ventured beneath the umbrella to ask me to go swimming, my mother would indignantly point at the book she'd just shoved into my hand. "She can't. She's reading." Actually I was relieved she butted in, since I didn't know how to swim anyway.

The nineties arrived like a blessing. I could start sweating again. I wanted to make up for all the sweating I'd missed out on. "Easy does it, though, Oca," my father told me.

Then one day in late June, just as the elation of spending a summer in a swimsuit on the beach was about to open wide before me, I got back home leaving a trail of blood by the door. I leaned over to find out where it had come from and discovered that a piece of glass had gotten lodged in my shoe and my foot.

"We've reached the height of paradox," my father said.

To him, we were always reaching the height of paradox. It was never clear what the paradox consisted of, but we had definitely reached it.

He removed the piece of glass and returned threateningly with his roll of paper towels. He drenched some with alcohol to disinfect my foot. "I knew you'd end up with tetanus."

To keep tetanus, or anything else, from eating away at my whole body, after the alcohol came the fire. My father grabbed a pair of scissors, heated them over the stove until they were glowing hot, and cauterized the wound directly. The mark is still there today. It looks like a heart-shaped wart, and the sight of it still moves me.

It's the only scar I have from my youth. We like to imagine, to talk about our bodies as a historical map of a disaster zone, but given that I skipped the customary childhood traumas—falls from trees, from bicycles, from roller skates— all I have is that tiny heart on the bottom of my foot to remind me that I was once a young girl.

The looming threat of perspiration was replaced by the danger of shards of glass on the street, a danger even more insidious than syringes, because it was unpredictable. Avoiding playgrounds, dark alleys, and porticoes wasn't enough. Shards of glass were everywhere. Shards of glass were as inescapable as entropy.

After that I was no longer allowed to wear shoes with rubber soles, only leather ones. Even on the beach. In fact, especially on the beach, where it was impossible to know whether a little piece of glass might be lurking beneath the sand. I spent the summer in a bathing suit and leather boots (two sizes too big, so you could easily shove a bunch of insoles into them, just to be on the safe side).

Now it was me who didn't want me to leave the umbrella. I discovered an unexplored world more captivating than the deep blue sea. Rebuses, barred crosswords, Edgar Allan Poe stories, solitaire.

Around other kids, at that point I figured I might as well lay claim to my eccentricity. "Yeah, sure, I'm wearing boots at the beach. So what? Can you solve *Susi's Queries* in *La Settimana Enigmistica*?"

That was the summer I read more books than my brother. The summer I consistently beat my father at briscola. The summer I sacrificed myself for the *poètes maudits* and Lovecraft. Other summers would arrive, imperturbably identical to one another. But not me! I worked long and hard on forcing my style to fit that single fundamental aspect of my life: my leather boots. I walked around in the sweltering Rome August like a dandy in the London fog. I went through a grunge, existentialist phase. Then a Jean Seberg phase. But actually it was that summer that Susi, with her striped shirt, hands in her pockets, and pointy breasts, forever forged my ideal of sex appeal.

*   *   *

And then there was the summer of Ventotene.

That is, the summer we didn't go to Ventotene.

My mother had started planning our summer vacations following the advice of an education magazine whose summer issue included a few ads for hotels on the seaside or in the mountains.

She was convinced that vacationing at one of those hotels would give her the chance to meet teachers like her and, consequently, would ensure that her children would make friends with the children of other teachers and would maybe start dating the children of other teachers and then in turn become teachers who would one day spawn new children of teachers to then forever spend their vacations and their lives all together in a pedagogical loop. To her, that was the life.

That year, the magazine that inspired her dream vacations led her to the island of Ventotene. She couldn't swim, but that didn't matter; breathing in the iodine was good for the health. I never knew if my father could swim. He said he could, but I never saw him go into the water past his knees. For the most part he stayed fully dressed at the café at the beach, smoking MS cigarettes from seven in the morning on.

Before the trip, my parents fought nonstop. To my father it sounded like torture, being stuck on an island: "We've reached the height of paradox." My mother shifted from resentment to a flash depression and withdrew to her bed. "All right, it doesn't matter . . ." she would moan every morning, and then lie there all day listening to Radio 3.

If I have one image of my mother during my childhood, it's this: she's in bed with a headband on because of her migraine, listening to Radio 3. When she got up she would put a deep-red acrylic robe on over her nightgown and wander the living room.

She never spoke of depression. Her headaches had a mystical quality to them but were of prosaic origins: they might be brought on by a self-diagnosed yet untreated sinus infection, secondhand smoke, an argument with my father, or concern for her children. When she was gripped by these migraines, every particle of her body emanated a mist of malaise into the air. The shutters of all the windows were rolled down, and my brother and I had to live in the half darkness and not make a sound. Our home became a hazy swamp of anguish where from time to time my mother's robe would drift into view like a reddish ghost, but the silence was warded off by the warm, velvety voices of the announcers on Radio 3.

Ever since my brother and I began to be published, the only moments my mother takes our profession seriously are when we're invited on the show *Fahrenheit*. For a couple years now she's even started calling them obsessively to take part in their on-air quizzes.

"We've got Francesca on the phone," announces the familiar voice on Radio 3. "Tell us, what do you think today's mystery book is?"

My mother blurts out a random title just so she can get to the highlight of her call.

"I'm Christian and Verika's mother!"

At that point, they hang up on her.

Anyway, that same summer, my father had been given a company car. Since he was the head of human resources, during the Christmas holidays we were used to getting packages from new hires or their relatives who wanted to express their gratitude.

The mountain of presents was stacked neatly by the door and then returned to the senders as soon as the flow of donations stopped pouring in. That was what my father thought was the life: never asking for and never accepting anything from anyone.

I always burst into tears when I got home and found the foyer empty, though naturally at the time I wouldn't have known what to do with a bottle of armagnac or a silver cigarette lighter case.

Nevertheless, he'd been forced to accept the company car. Which was humiliating: his old Opel Kadett didn't meet his company's standards. We were poorer than someone in his job was expected to be, and rather than opting for a more logical solution like giving him a raise, they'd gone with a riskier, counterintuitive solution: we'd been allowed to stay poorer but with a car for the wealthy.

As it turned out, my mother's martyrdom worked and my father gave in to the idea of going to Ventotene. My brother and I were overjoyed, because it would be our first trip in the company car. The first trip with air conditioning and electric windows.

We lived in a tall building just next to the tenements of Ponte Mammolo and Rebibbia, a complex that was basically identical to them but, unlike the tenements, boasted a layer of grass covering the roof of the parking garage, pruned oleander shrubs, and an automatic sliding gate intended to simulate a measure of protection for members of the middle class with a company car.

The morning of our departure, we got all comfy in the seats that still had that new-car smell and immediately turned on the air conditioning. We drove up the ramp leading to the automatic gate, which started to open but then suddenly changed its mind, snapping shut like a mischievous theater curtain. We crashed into it, totaling the hood of the car.

That was how that summer we ended up stuck not on an island but inside our apartment, without even the car. My parents didn't speak to each other, my mother didn't once take off her robe even though it was a hundred degrees out, my brother and I learned to make saliva bubbles on the tips of our tongues and spit them at each other.

The name Ventotene became taboo and no one dared utter it ever again.

A couple years ago I was invited to a literary festival on Ventotene.

Over twenty years had gone by since our accident with the gate, and yet I had never happened to go there.

While on the ferry, I thought about how I would've liked to tell my father about it. I would've liked to call him to crack a stupid joke and remind him about the incident and all the money we had to shell out to fix our fancy car without his company finding out.

I don't remember exactly when it was that I stopped thinking about my father every day after his death. Sooner or later it happened, like it does after a relationship ends. You think it's not possible, but it is. The moment arrives. But in the months before the festival, the thought of him came back all over again as part of my nightly insomnia.

It was a thought stranger than it was painful. I was about to turn forty and it felt weird to think of him imagining anything of the sort. Nine years had gone by since his death, and my life hadn't changed much. I was doing the same things I'd done when he was alive—I couldn't sleep, got pissed off for the same reasons. Despite my promises to him, I continued to smoke and no one had ever given me a company car, since I had neither a company nor a driver's license anyway (another broken promise, that one day I'd get one).

One thing had radically changed, though: I'd stopped feeling like a daughter. And in those months leading up to my birthday I thought of how much I would've liked to feel like one again.

I don't know why when I imagine talking to my father there's always a telephone separating us. We never had long phone conversations, but I end up missing the sound of his voice more than his physical presence, so my brain mentally dials his number, which I've never forgotten. That still happens to me today: without realizing it, I memorize numbers that are important to me and it's impossible to remove them from my mental contact list, even if I try.

What would I have said to him? "Papà, I'm about to turn forty. Can you believe it?"

"Yes, Oca. We've reached the height of paradox."

It was the first time I had distinct memories of him when he was my age. I wished I could talk to him about it on the phone, about how surprising it was to reach the same age as the image I had of him, to compare myself to that image.

My feelings were mixed: I wanted to feel like a daughter again but also finally like an adult during an age of his life I could remember.

During the literary festival, when my mother called to remind me to breathe in the iodine in the early morning hours and not to stay out in the sun at noon, I wondered what effect it had on her that I was on Ventotene, whether she remembered that summer of resentment holed up at home in debt because of the company car. I was tempted to ask her, but was afraid of having to face all her repressed memories. "Oh, please! What are you talking about? We ended up going to San Benedetto del Tronto," is what she would've told me, or something like that. Then she would've changed the subject. "Don't drink too much, it's bad for you." So I didn't bother asking her.

But as I stayed out in the sun during the worst hours of the day instead of breathing in the morning iodine, I imagined my father there on the island. And I missed his nervousness, how uncomfortable he would have felt in a place so resistant to his control freakery, all the awkwardness that would have turned into a bad temper. I knew his vacation on Ventotene would have been a living hell, that he would have been without his natural habitat full of asphalt and protection, the pleasure of hopping into the car to go buy the paper. He would have forced me and my brother to walk around in hiking boots, not as much because of shards of glass, but because he would never have believed the islanders' reassurances that there weren't any snakes. Then he would have stuck a K-Way windbreaker over our swimsuits to protect us from the sea breeze. He would have kept us kilometers away from rocky walls that at any moment might have crumbled and buried us alive. Because the water wasn't potable, he would have kept us from eating fruit and vegetables and probably everything else, and we'd have ended up living off of canned tuna and crackers and brushing our teeth with bottles of Ferrarelle. Sooner or later he would have made up some emergency at work to go home ahead of schedule, loading the family and the luggage into the company car, heading toward the muggy comfort of a deserted Rome where he could drive around aimlessly in the car, just to enjoy being shut up inside it, sheltered from the elements.

The car has since passed down to A., and now it looks nothing like a company car. Our friends have nicknamed it "the Swedish Beater," and it seems so shady and out of place on the streets of the Pigneto district, amid the bicycles, Rollerblades, vans, and Car2Go Smart cars. It's become a community vehicle; there's always someone borrowing it to move, for a trip out of town, or because of some emergency. Inside is an accumulated legacy left behind by those who've passed through: a scarf, a hat, a pizza box, a copy of *Internazionale*, lots of cigarette lighters and packets of tissues bought from peddlers at traffic lights. The chrome plating has grown dull and dusty, changed from silver to antique gray, the upholstery is torn up, the fabric has detached from the inside roof and sags down like an unfurled flag. It looks like the car of penniless drug dealers waiting to expand their business so they can afford something better.

I know how maniacal my father was with the car, like he was with everything else, but the Beater doesn't make me think of him anymore, or of Ventotene, or of my parents' arguments with Mina or Mia Martini singing in the background on the radio. It doesn't make me think of anything. Not even my own memories. Trips with A., or the moving boxes loaded into it when I left home. To me it's just the Swedish Beater, and anyone can take it and leave something behind in it, spill a beer, have a cry or a heart-wrenching phone call with the fabric dangling down on top of their head. It'll keep getting older, and the antique gray will become even more antique, a patina of deterioration that nostalgia does nothing to improve, and it'll break down and will one day end up at the junkyard, and there definitely won't be anyone going to visit it or bring it flowers, but maybe there'll be someone who needs an engine or a door. How I wish the past always worked like that.

U ntil I was nineteen I didn't sleep with anyone. Well, that's not exactly true, but I'll get back to that later.

All the times I fell in love it was completely platonic. It's no coincidence my name can be anagrammed to "I crave no *amori*." Not physically, that is.

In the summer before sixth grade, when I was living swaddled in paper towels, I spent a good chunk of the vacation in my room spying on a boy as he read on the balcony of the hotel across from us. The fact that he was reading didn't make him fascinating to me as much as it made me recognize him as a fellow junkie. I was a young girl, while he couldn't have been a minor, because he had a car, was on his own, and had come from Germany (the license plate on his car was from Aachen, as I learned from my brother, who'd memorized the license plate codes of all the European cities).

One day, when I'd stayed out late alone on the beach, contemplating the sun setting on the horizon, I saw him literally walking out of the water. I was speechless as I beheld his silhouette slowly rising against the red of the sky, halfway between Venus and Christ. I'd been there staring at the sea for hours and was sure he'd never gone into the water. He only emerged from it. I told myself I had known the Absolute.

That's what I told the other girls in class when I went back to school in September.

"So, what'd you do this summer?"

"I knew the Absolute."

I took out the phone book and looked up the number of the auto registration offices in Rome, hoping to track down the offices in Aachen, but unfortunately I found out that knowing the license plate of the Absolute won't help you reach the Absolute.

In eighth grade I fell in love with Laszlo, a homeless Polish man who begged outside the supermarket. I would go with my mother to do the shopping, and in the paper cup he kept out for change I left a series of notes filled with love for his clear, kind eyes. One day he reciprocated with a note for me. On it was written a place and time to meet. Telling my mother I was going to a classmate's to study, I went to meet Laszlo at the park. He said "Hello" and "How are you?" to me many times, to which I replied politely. Then we stayed there for a long time looking into each other's eyes. He pulled out another note. Written on it was: "*I love you. You have money?*" Before I could draw a connection between the two concepts, my mother appeared out of nowhere.

"Hello," Laszlo said to her. "How are you?"

My mother dragged me home and changed supermarkets.

That summer I fell in love with Diego, a boy who was about ten years older than me and who at the end of vacation brushed me off with a classic I'll-Be-Back-When-You've-Grown-Up letter.

In September I began to take the Cattell intelligence tests my brother used to get into Mensa. I didn't make the minimum score of 148, so I couldn't have become a Mensan, but still I had a much higher than average IQ.

I wrote Diego a letter explaining that he didn't need to go anywhere, because I was already grown up. He never replied.

In freshman year of high school it was the turn of a young Russian poet I met at a poetry slam. He'd come by bus from Moscow just to read his verses in Russian while a wonky translation in Italian was projected onto a screen behind him. He came in last place in the slam.

I walked up to him at the end of the performance. His English was decent, mine wasn't. The next morning he was taking the bus back to Moscow. I watched him head off with a company of poets to a nearby pizzeria.

He was short, had long hair, and wore an overcoat a Beckettian vagrant might wear. (I had never seen Laszlo, who actually was a vagrant, wear an overcoat, only down jackets by Fila or Sergio Tacchini.)

The next morning I cut class and went to the bus station. The young Russian poet ran to embrace me. He had deep green eyes I hadn't noticed the night before and breath that wafted the powerful smell of beer into the cloudless sky over the Tiburtina station.

"Come with me," he said. I stared at him. He was serious. I had proof too: here was a guy who'd spent over two days on a bus so he could read verses at a poetry slam and come in last. "You can start a new life for yourself in Moscow."

I thought about the possibility like my mother thought about her army of never-born babies. I continued to think about it even after he left. Though I never started a new life for myself in Moscow, I'll forever be grateful to the young Russian poet for making it seem, for a few months at least, like a possibility.

I never received a sexual education. My mother used to tell me that when she kept trying and failing to get pregnant, she would stare resentfully at other women's big bellies and have the urge to pop them with a pin. When I was little I thought that was how it really worked, that a pin was enough to make those bloated bellies deflate. I imagined them suddenly bursting on a tram, at a café table, in the frozen foods aisle. I pictured the incredulous women turning over in their hands a strange mass, at that point similar to pizza dough. Before finally conceiving my brother and ceasing to plot voodoo rituals against womankind, my mother never thought of going to the doctor to check whether everything was working correctly. Neither had my father, for that matter: "Be serious. Like I would go there to jack off."

She told me this recently, and it surprised me to hear her use that expression, "jack off," though she said it as though it were a technical term. Anyway, at first I didn't get why she'd decided to tell me the story, but then it became clear.

"So don't you give up."

"Mamma, I'm not trying to have children."

"It doesn't matter. Don't give up anyway."

My mother took her periods as a monthly defeat, my father's "Well, we'll see" drowning in blood. On the days she
had them she would stay in bed not because of cramps but
because of her deep despondency. She would turn on Radio
3 and think about her army of never-born babies. At times I
thought about them too. I wondered what it would've been
like to live with a dozen siblings in a sixty-square-meter
apartment, which at that point would've become a beehive
thanks to my father's walls, each of us holed up in our tiny
cell of the honeycomb to avoid disturbing the sacred despondency of the queen bee immersed in the buzz of the radio.

Apulian folklore had also developed a hearty collection of
superstitions about menstruation: when you had your period
you couldn't cut your hair because it would never grow back;
you couldn't water plants because they would self-combust;
and you couldn't pour milk because it would curdle in the
glass. All you could do was abandon yourself to boredom
and the thought of never-born babies.

I was in eighth grade when I had my first period—the last
girl in my class to get it—and my mother personally took me
to school and explained to all the teachers, including Don
Serafino, my temporarily hindered state.

At seventeen I told her I wanted to see a gynecologist and
she took it as a provocation.

That afternoon she phoned all her friends so they would know to what lengths my turbulent adolescent restlessness had driven me.

"Where did I go wrong? There was a time when she simply liked to draw."

I have no idea how her friends reacted, but it didn't matter, seeing how for my mother phone conversations worked like forty-minute-long voicemail messages.

That night, my father was also informed of the scandal.

"Your daughter wants to see a gynecologist."

"We've reached the height of paradox."

I never had any real reason to see a gynecologist apart from the fact that all the other girls in my class were going. A gynecologist seemed like a figure who appeared in a girl's life to unequivocally mark her having crossed the threshold into puberty. The other girls went to the beautician too, had their hair layered by hairdressers, and some had even started getting French manicures, not long before Chanel's *rouge noir* nail polish forever tarnished the hands of girls around the world. I bit my nails and had the peach fuzz of a newborn, and my father would cut my hair with disposable Gillette razors.

In my neighborhood there was a tall girl dressed in black who I always saw going around on her own. She looked more like a vestal virgin in some dark ritual than a banal goth girl, though to be fair the goths in the northeast outskirts of Rome in the nineties were practically nonexistent—either there simply weren't any or they were staying holed up somewhere. I was fascinated by her and always hoped that somehow we would meet.

One day I gathered my courage and struck up a conversation with her while we were waiting at a crosswalk. It turned out we lived just a few blocks from each other. Before we even became friends, she passed by our place one night to bring me a pot of *crema pasticcera* spiked with rum because she'd heard I was running a fever. I spent the night in bed, pleasantly hammered.

Who knows why, but my father instantly took a liking to her. "The beanstalk's nice."

Her name was Francesca, but she'd decided to change it to Glenda. "Everyone's already got a Francesca in their life," she explained. Who could disagree?

It turns out Glenda's mother was a gynecologist.

That was how I went for my first secret checkup. She discovered I had a cyst in my breast that needed urgent removal.

I didn't know how to pass the information on to my parents.

"Who felt you up?" was my mother's reaction.

The fact that it was the beanstalk's mother helped calm their outrage, but I could never confess she'd also put me on the pill to regulate my period, given that I only got it a couple times a year. My mother had never taken the pill. She described in horror the time she'd seen a girl pull it out of her purse on a bus. It was as if she'd caught her fingering herself in public.

My parents took me to the hospital to have the cyst removed. Before I was taken into the operating room, my father disinfected me from head to toe with rubbing alcohol. "Be careful, Oca," he said. "Don't touch anything."

Once inside, as the anesthetic was starting to kick in, the last thing I heard from behind the mask of the doctor who was about to cut open my breast was, "Sorry, but this won't make them any bigger . . ."

I drifted off to sleep, picturing nonna Muccia high-fiving him.

Six years ago I went back to that same hospital to terminate a pregnancy.

It was the year when lots of people I knew were having children or discovering they had celiac disease.

In both cases it was hard to have anything to do with them without their dragging you into one of the two topics with proselytic zeal. Especially hard to crack a joke or not show due interest. Having children or eliminating gluten from one's diet meant a radical change in lifestyle. Everything led

back to that foundational turning point in their experience. I
was surrounded by people who had been completely reborn,
capable of distinguishing their existence into a before and an
after. The children that had established new priorities and
ambitions, given new meaning to the concept of joy; the
gluten-free diet that had resolved every imaginable symp-
tom: insomnia, anxiety, headaches, constipation.

Personally, I had all those symptoms, which weren't very
different from the ones caused by anemia or microcytosis,
but I refused to be tested, preferring to think of myself as
a person with a bad attitude. I guess it was because of my
laziness, my indolence, as always.

For the same reason, after being late for a number of
days—I couldn't have said how many because I never kept
track of my menstrual cycle—I didn't bother to buy a pregnancy test just to dispel any doubt. With a certain overcon-
fidence, I didn't "feel pregnant," and since all the women I
knew had told me about that strange awareness of "feeling
pregnant" the moment they actually became pregnant, I
settled for it as proof. Later I would discover that that awareness was for the most part the result of meticulous calcula-
tions, months of attempts, obsessively keeping track of their
hormonal fluctuations. I bought a pregnancy test almost
entirely because Cristina, a friend of mine from Berlin, kept
pestering me about it.

"Still late?"

"Yes."

"So why don't you buy a test?"

It was one of the two: either I stopped talking to Cristina or I had to buy a test, because I didn't know how to answer her.

Not to minimize my friend's thoughtfulness, but it also should be said that in Berlin you can find pregnancy tests at supermarkets in baskets by the cash register, and you can buy one for three euros. At the first pharmacy I walked into in Rome, they only sold a two-pack at the price of twenty-one euros. In the second pharmacy there was a single pack, and it cost fourteen euros.

"How is this possible? What good is the European Community?" I grumbled.

The third pharmacy sold single packs—on sale—at nine euros. An opportunity not to be missed.

I'd spent the morning at a café editing a story I'd written for an anthology by women writers on the topic of biological clocks. In the story was this line written in the third person about the main character: "Like all young women who had never used contraception, she'd convinced herself she was sterile."

Though I was satisfied with my story, I harbored doubts about the anthology. Banal doubts: the self-seclusion of women writers made to express their opinion on a "female" topic.

Anyway, to establish a timeline, at around twelve thirty I finished editing the story and emailed it in. I ordered a glass of prosecco, because whenever I turn something in I need one of my little celebratory rituals. At one I bought the test at the pharmacy. At one thirty I put a pot of water on the stove. When the water reached a boil I slid an egg into it and went to pee on the test stick.

Though I always tend to waste a bunch of time, I hate having to wait, so I try to fill that time when I can. In the five minutes it took the egg to cook, the test would be ready too. I removed the egg from the water and read the results: pregnant.

I didn't know who to tell. Glenda's mother had retired. I called her anyway. She was happy to hear from me and asked what I was writing. She always read my books. Then, without my even bringing up the subject, she asked, "Know who the father is?"

Her question made me laugh, but I really appreciated it. She explained what I had to do.

I've never spoken to my mother about the abortion, but I think she would take it as some kind of sick joke. A jab said just to get back at her for the constant supply of onesies and rompers. On the other hand, if she took it seriously, it would only signify a new recruit in her army of never-born babies.

For once, my brother spared me the parables and gave me a book instead: *Why Have Children?* by Christine Overall. I told him it seemed somewhat inappropriate, given that I'd already come to a decision.

"No, no, that's beside the point. It's a good work of non-fiction, so well written."

A month later he gave me two essays by Melanie Klein: "Criminal Tendencies in Normal Children" and "On the Theory of Anxiety and Guilt," because they too were so well written. But he did take me at five in the morning to get in line outside the basement level of the hospital ward where abortions were performed, in one of my three attempts to start the whole process. The night before, incredibly, it had snowed in Rome, and at dawn I found myself in the middle of a cluster of women clutching plastic cups of boiling-hot coffee and stale glazed cornetti.

Before the procedure I waited on an examination table next to a Ukrainian woman who barely spoke Italian, but I think neither of us felt like chatting to pass the time. She offered me a slice of lemon to wet my lips, since we couldn't drink water. It was a simple gesture, and just then it was all I could have wanted.

When the procedure was over, A. was there waiting for me in the waiting room. Then we went to lunch by the sea. At least, that was the plan. It turned out the restaurants on the beach were all closed. We ended up getting a couple slices of pizza and eating them on the shore beneath the February sun. When I turned my phone back on, notifications of my mother's calls came in. Then the stream of texts: *"Hey there"*, *"How are you?"*, *"What are you doing?"*, *"Why won't*

you answer?", "*Text me*", "*Where are you?*", "*What's going on?*",
"*Text me*", "*Text me*", "*Why won't you talk to your mother?*",
"*Why are you doing this to me?*", "*Are you bickering with A.?*",
"*Text me*", "*What happened?*", "*Text me.*"

A. showed me his phone: "*Why isn't my daughter answering me?*", "*Why aren't you two answering me?*", "*Have you been
bickering?*", "*Why won't anyone talk to me?*", "*What's going
on?*", "*Text me*", "*What did I do?*"

Eventually my mother's messages regressed. They stopped
being articulate, lost their phonemes, and became a jumble
of graphic symbols: "*??!*c§+.*"

I called her back. You could hear the strong wind blowing
across the beach.

"Always out living it up, aren't you?" she said.

When I went back to the hospital for the follow-up visit
there was a different doctor than the one who'd operated on
me. He was a man in his sixties, one of those sporty types,
distinguished graying hair, who always look like they've just
finished playing a tennis match. He seemed not at all happy
to be there. I even less than him. From my file he read my
year of birth: "Nineteen seventy-eight." He enunciated the
number as if revealing something I didn't know. I just nodded
as he remained absorbed in his personal Kabbalah.

"You're not so young," he said.

"Okay," I said.

"Why'd you decide to abort?"

I thought I'd been spared that kind of question, given that I'd skipped the optional psych consult before the procedure, but evidently I'd flunked a test somewhere along the line, and was now being given an oral exam.

"Because I didn't want to have a child," I answered.

This time it was he who nodded. We were sitting there stating the obvious to each other, a postmatch pastime.

"You're not a little girl," he told me. "If you don't want to have a child, you should know what to do to avoid it."

It struck me that at least his comment about my not being so young anymore made sense now. But there was more to it.

"You realize this could've been your last chance?"

The light from a lethargic sun was coming in through the window. All I wanted was to get out of that room. Be done with all the other last chances awaiting me. Miss trains, not seize moments, burn bridges and the candle at both ends, wallow in a sea of the irreversible.

The doctor examined me. There was nothing irregular.

"When can I have intercourse again?" I asked.

"That's all you can think about, huh?"

I could report him for this, I told myself, but then a memory made me follow another course of action.

In high school, Madame Perillo, the French teacher who boasted that she had perfect pronunciation because she'd never been to France, where it would've been negatively influenced by the natives, loved to tell us over and over that we were "a bunch of failures." Whenever someone pronounced something wrong or stated that "*La* stylo est sur *le* table" rather than "*Le* stylo est sur *la* table," she would remind us of our collective identity: "a bunch of failures." Not that we had any objection to it. At that age it seemed more appealing to us to pass ourselves off as existential failures than to correctly guess the gender of a French noun.

One day in sophomore year, Madame Perillo called me up to the board to conjugate the verb *choisir*. It wasn't a stellar performance, and she sent me back to my desk with the familiar shadow of failure looming over me. At that point something happened that never actually happened: Madame Perillo heard me say, "The truth is, is that we only care about fucking."

I really wished I'd had the swagger, the guts to utter anything of the sort, not to mention at least a shred of personal experience to make it believable, but I found myself in the embarrassing situation of not even being able to brag about it to my classmates, given that they were all witnesses to my silent return to my desk. Nevertheless, Madame Perillo was utterly convinced it happened, and she called an extraordinary faculty meeting. While the teachers quietly discussed what to do, me and the bunch of other failures prepared our defense. What was more dignified: Pretending I'd said it? Claiming it as a slogan, or fighting for the truth?

It all concluded with a humiliating telling off by the teachers.

"Kids, kids . . . What do you want to make of your lives?"

Actually, none of them even cared whether the remark had been said or not. All they cared about was hearing a collective retraction of the ideals it expressed.

Years later, in that visiting room at the hospital, I decided to stand up for the teenager I had been along with the entire bunch of failures.

"The truth is, is that we only care about fucking," I said, feeling a bit at fault for the use of a reduplicative copula.

Only recently did I discover that I needed to add another cemetery to the list of those I continue to ignore: "the fetus graveyard," or, to call it by the euphemism used by the Catholic associations that run places like it, "the angel garden." Actually, I didn't even know such a thing existed until this year, when I read an article in the paper in which a woman reported having found her first and last name written on a cross. Buried beneath the cross was the fetus she'd aborted.

The woman had had the procedure at my hospital and had never authorized a burial. She wrote a post on Facebook describing what had happened. Other accounts followed from women who discovered the same thing: a cross with their first and last name and the date of the abortion.

Beneath the crosses were the remains of their embryos or fetuses. They'd never given their authorization, or at least to their knowledge hadn't done so. Had I? I had no idea. Had I been asked? Had I signed something? The truth is I'd never wondered in the slightest what happened to the "conception material." I'd never even heard the term before, and reading it like that, it might have even seemed like a good book title.

I finished reading the article, did a bit of research online, and called A. I told him what I'd discovered.

"Sounds like a horror movie," he said.

Instead it was just the Italian right wing teaming up with antiabortion Catholicism. Which, in fact, were two perfect ingredients for a horror movie.

"Think we should go see for ourselves?" I asked him.

"What do you want to do?"

I didn't know what to say. I was outraged, furious, shocked, but didn't feel the opening of old wounds, didn't feel a surge of grief. What kind of experience would it be, going there and discovering a cross? The first thing I thought was that I didn't know of any bars near the cemetery where I could go afterwards to drink. It's hard for me to think of facing an important experience without a bar nearby. Besides, was it really important?

A while back, a girlfriend of mine asked me, "So why do Italian novels always talk about family bonds?"

Given that in that period I was in the process of writing this book, I gracefully skirted the issue. But then came the second zinger.

"And someone's always mourning. It's like they're the first ones to ever discover death."

I laughed the sheepish laugh of someone caught red-handed.

A. and I decided not to go to the "angel garden." For a while I continued to follow the news about the ongoing investigation into the case, given that apart from the bad taste it was a violation of privacy. Then I stopped doing even that. But today, thinking back on what my friend said, I've told myself that in a way she had a point. Sometimes we write not to process grief, but to make it up.

One afternoon, a few months before my father got sick, a few months before there was any suspicion he would, I ran into an old classmate on the street, a guy I hadn't seen for a long time. We'd never been close friends, he was barely more than a stranger I had nothing to say to. The cheerful smile on his face as he walked up to me threw me into a panic. It made me uncomfortable, his body, his gaze, the glow of his skin, the garish color of his sneakers. His presence requiring mine. The idea of striking up a conversation there on the sidewalk or exchanging a kiss on the cheek. Small talk

frightens me, makes me feel exposed, like I'm running behind in life: I'm aware I lack the rudiments and the practice.
The same thing happens to me with analog clocks. I can't
read the hands, have never figured out how they work. One
of the last things my father asked me was what time it was.
We were in the hospital and his gold watch was sitting on
the bedside table—that is, right before my eyes—but I had
to pull my cell phone out of my purse.

"Oca, I can't believe it. You still haven't learned?"

That time I didn't hear him say "We've reached the height
of paradox." Maybe with the end drawing near, things seemed
less irrational to him. Maybe ceasing to exist made all other
paradoxes pale in comparison.

After my father died, I put his gold watch around my wrist,
both because it was a memento, and because I thought it
looked nice. If someone on the street asked me what time
it was, I would thrust my arm out and plant the watch face
right under their nose. But if that turned out to be too
complicated—let's say the person asking was too far away
from me—I would hurry my step and pretend I hadn't heard
them, or simply shrug my shoulders sadly: "Sorry, I no speak
Italian."

My old classmate breezed along, his smile unwavering,
convincing: he was good, knew what he was doing. Rudiments and the practice. "It's been ages! How's it going?"

"My father died," I said.

I don't know why I did it. Maybe just to get out of the embarrassing need to say something. The only time I've ever managed to utter that sentence so clearly was right then, when my father was still peacefully alive. And yet I felt all the dismay over his death. My friend withdrew his smile and I, unable to take back my lie, began to tell him about what I hadn't yet experienced with the same meticulousness with which my mother describes the torture her son is being subjected to in a parking garage in Rome. My friend had never faced such a serious loss, he told me, but recently his dog had died. His dog for fifteen years, a mutt, a lifelong companion. We talked about hospitals and veterinary clinics. Good doctors and bad ones. Empathy and cynicism. Burial and cremation. Sleepless nights and the need to start afresh. I fished out images and emotions from movies I'd seen, books I'd read. The absurdity of it all disarmed my discomfort. I began to weep. At that point the loss of my father had become implacable. I could've written a novel about it. In the end he hugged me. By then his body had become tolerable— anyone's body would have been, human touch in a desolate wasteland. He said he remembered my father. It was meant to be an affectionate remark, but I sensed a hint of uneasiness. I think Papà had shouted in his face too.

Glenda's mother was not only my secret gynecologist but also the only adult woman I could talk to about sex. At age nineteen, when I became sexually active, I could go to her place to fuck. She covered with my parents, and if Francesca was on the phone, she stalled her while I was busy in the other room.

Za and I got back together after years of having lost touch. He was more embarrassed than me when we came out of the bedroom and joined Glenda and her mother in the kitchen to open a bottle of wine, but the alternative to that embarrassment would've been finding a basement, a stairwell, some bushes, a car we could borrow.

To be exact, when I say nineteen it's a symbolic number, one I chose just to have an anniversary in mind, given my lack of solid evidence. I'd ended up in bed with boys before then but, having no idea what fucking meant, I didn't think that was what was happening, though today it's hard to imagine what kind of out-of-body experience I was undergoing at those particular moments. I don't think it was as much a question of poor physical performance by the other party as it was my own cognitive deficit. I didn't feel what I should've felt because I didn't know what it was I should've been feeling.

The concept of "letting yourself go" has always been foreign to me for a very banal reason: I don't understand where it is I'm supposed to go.

To me, every experience needs a precise linguistic or empirical explanation, an illustrated primer complete with examples; otherwise I'm oblivious to the fact that I'm experiencing it. The same thing happened with alcohol and weed. Until it was explained to me that drinking or smoking got you high, how the process occurred, what effects I was supposed to feel, until I saw them occurring in my drinking companions and they explicitly asked me to join in, I could easily have ingested any amount of any substance without feeling the slightest bit different.

There was something ineffable even about physical pain. I remember one afternoon when I was little and I hit my head against a corner. I stood there, blood trickling steadily down my face. When my mother saw me, she shrieked. "Good lord, what did you do to yourself?"

What had I done to myself? With a delayed reaction, I cried for a good hour, only because at that point it seemed like the most appropriate thing to do.

Anyway, after Za left me for Anastasia, I began to harbor the secret longing that one day I would run into him again, and I vowed he would be my first. And so, when I actually did run into him again, I was convinced I was still a virgin. And I kept on being convinced of it even during our many secret rendezvous in the garage of his building. One afternoon, as we were undoing our jeans, I told him, "I'm ready."

He looked at me, not understanding.

"I've decided I want to make love."

He continued to not understand.

"I want to lose my virginity. To you."

At that point he looked vaguely alarmed.

"But Smilzi, we've already fucked."

I hadn't realized. He asked me how many other people I *hadn't* fucked before him, but that escaped me too. It still escapes me today. There are at least a couple episodes that raise my suspicion: for example, a guy from Stockholm who afterwards remarked, "Nice fuck." The use of the word "nice" rather than "good" or "great" made me think it was a euphemism to tell me, "Sorry, it didn't work." And then there was a skeletal DJ who kept making this deathly, tormented sound as he slammed his hips against me, and that time I'm really not sure what we did, because I was too frightened by that sensation of an ossuary coming to life against me. I never worked up the nerve to ask for elucidation, nor did I ever work up the nerve to ask Glenda's mother whether she realized what was going on but was waiting for me to figure it out on my own.

*   *   *

One weekend I told my parents I'd be staying over at Glenda's, and instead Za and I drove off to Ascoli Piceno, where my father had bought a house. It was his hometown, and he wanted it to become the cozy little hideaway where he'd spend his old age. Meanwhile, he went there to build walls, since there wasn't room for any more of them in our apartment in Rome. Sometimes my mother went with him, but usually she preferred to stay in bed, despondently listening to Radio 3. My brother and I had never cared about the house, but now that we were both looking for a place to fuck, we made our timid requests. My father simply ignored them. "Well, we'll see . . ." he said. And so once again I'd been forced to steal something from his dresser—this time, the keys.

Za borrowed a car and we headed off for our fiery weekend of sex. It would be the first time we'd be sleeping together. For me it would also be the first time I'd ever slept in a bed with a man, other than my grandpa. On the way there we had all the time we wanted to dream up a repertory of erotic fantasies to squeeze into under forty-eight hours, now that I understood how things worked.

Having reached the place in Ascoli, we should've raced up the stairs, burst through the door, and torn off each other's clothes, but instead, for no real reason, I stopped by the mailbox and slid my hand into the slot, which was big enough for my slender fingers. I rummaged around and fished out an electricity bill and three letters for my father.

The address was written in what I without hesitation would define as a feminine hand.

While Za waited for me by the bedroom, I put a pot of water on to boil.

"What are you doing?"

In Mickey Mouse comics I'd read that envelopes could be opened using steam.

We spent the night fighting. He thought it was crazy for me to want to read my father's mail. I thought it was crazy that my father had bought a house in Ascoli where he could take his lover.

I pulled out the first letter. It was from Rosa.

I'd seen her only twice, at parties for employees and their families. She was about fifteen years younger than him and wasn't alluring. Neither was her letter, but it was full of affection. An affection I would never have imagined could seduce my father. At that age, I didn't yet know that caring for someone could be something so precious. It didn't fit into any of my categories.

I wasn't angry at the discovery that my father was cheating on my mother. I was simply disappointed by his choice. More than the banality of a manager screwing a coworker, I was disappointed by the banality of Rosa, her cutesy writing, her trite metaphors, her little essay on love. It was a bad letter, not a dirty one.

I wasn't even angry at the thought of my father getting back every night at ten, exhausted, short-tempered. In fact, suddenly all that dedication to work made sense. It was an even vaster form of company loyalty. I don't think Rosa was a distraction or the reason for my father being away from home. She was more like a harmonious element that made his workaholism tolerable. The months of unused vacation time, the Christmas Eves spent at the office, even his sense- less passion for building walls. I opened the second letter too, and by the third had already had enough.

Za and I managed to fuck only the next morning, badly, in a rush, under ice-cold sheets thanks to the house not having been heated for days. Then we were so depressed that we went out for breakfast in the square and decided to head back to Rome.

I've never known whether my father found out about my romantic getaway in Ascoli. No one ever made mention of it, and slowly what was left unsaid turned into something different, a complicity we refused to admit and which there- fore made us both closer and more distrustful.

I don't know how long his affair with Rosa lasted. A few years later she changed jobs, and yet my father's workaholism remained the same. Right up to the end. He didn't want to let his coworkers know he was sick until he had to go into the hospital. There he shaved every morning, daubed his mustache with a cork, and put on cologne. My brother and I had to monitor his visitors to keep anyone from the office from seeing him with stubble from the night before.

I never ran into Rosa at the hospital. I don't know if she went to visit him there. Afterwards, she sent a telegram with her condolences. Dry. Precise. Businesslike.

Za left me again a couple years later. This time I had been the one who left the country (I moved to Berlin) and cheated. With a tall guy. It couldn't have lasted, and in fact it didn't. But before I could even figure that out, Za came to visit me in Berlin with a marriage proposal, and he found out about the tall guy. He went back to Rome and within three months converted to Catholicism and got engaged to a girl who'd been presented to him directly by God. That happens to the newly converted—they have the tendency to interpret everything as a sign from the Lord.

Thinking back on it now, I'm amazed at how fast it all happened. My discovery of sex, the discovery of bodies, even tall ones, the discovery that fathers aren't the only ones who cheat, the discovery of a different city that would forever remain a place to return to during the imperfect escapes in my life. For someone else, the discovery of God.

I'd spent sleepless nights and years imagining a future with Za, and when that future arrived in the form of a proposal, I didn't know what to do with it. But I also didn't know what to do with the tall guy, whose biggest draw was his knowing how to light the coal stove in the apartment where I was living. He kept me warm, you could say. Actually, I liked to see him leaning over the little hatch when the flame was lit, his face illuminated by its red glow, the dramatic shadows cast on his back (he loved to do the chore bare-chested). I would watch him from the bed, in my apprenticeship in pleasure: every gesture was both erotic and ridiculous. D. H. Lawrence never mentions it, but I'm sure there must have been a moment when Lady Chatterley contemplates the gamekeeper's back only to find that her desire suddenly seems ludicrous.

When I tried to elaborate the concept with the tall guy, he had a hard time following me. Maybe it was because of my German, but more likely it was because he hated any interference with his vision of a bare-chested man who tames fire for a woman. There were other visions of himself he'd never doubted: he was a poet, he was a painter, he was a musician. A Renaissance man. Truth be told, he was also a scion of the Bavarian upper middle class. We drank champagne out of my coffee mugs. At the time I was a student who'd hung around to putz about in Berlin after Erasmus.

One day he rented a convertible and drove me to Munich to see the apartment he owned. His head stuck up over the top as he did over 190 kilometers an hour down the autobahn. He made a point of reminding me that in Germany there were no speed limits, saying it as though it had been his idea. He stopped to fill the tank with the same intensity with which he lit my fire. Finally we got to his place in down-town Munich: 160 square meters with stucco ceilings, his oil paintings on the walls (lots of bare-chested self-portraits), and a collection of Stratocasters.

"If you stay with me, all this will be yours," he said.

Men's generosity is immense, so incredibly immense that it always moves me. It's unfathomable what they offer com-pared to the little they ask in return. A disproportion that de-fies all laws of profit and leaves me utterly speechless. Like my brother's parables. The tall guy was willing to bestow upon me a home and numerous guitars (as for the self-portraits, we'd see) if only I stayed by his side.

I've met men even more generous than he was, actually. A politician offered me a salary as a parliamentary aide if I went to bed with him. He didn't even specify how many times—we hadn't gotten that far in the negotiations. Who knows? Maybe once would've been enough. Though his offer was already lavish, he also wanted me to rest assured about the fact that I'd receive the salary "without having to work a single day." A producer I met at a party instantly recognized my literary talent: "You can tell you know your stuff." He was a straightforward, intuitive man. At a glance he could spot a real writer, with no need to bother with the degrading formality of having to read her books. He was the most magnanimous of them all. He invited me to his office the next day. All he was asking for was fifteen minutes of my time, a blow job, that's

all—a nice, clean favor right there on the spot—and then
he'd grant me the opportunity to choose what to dedicate
my writing to: a drama series about a mother who was also
a traffic cop ("mother" came before "traffic cop") or a YA
show about teen werewolves.

After the Bavarian patron and I got back to Berlin—wind-
whipped hair, two hundred kilometers an hour, stopping
off to get gas while striking a pose—I slipped a note into his
mailbox: "*Thanks for everything. It's just that you're too tall.*"

The next day I decided to head back to Rome. I could've
taken advantage of the generosity of another man, my father, and had him buy me a last-minute plane ticket, but
I listened carefully to my inner voice and heard it say that
prodigal-son-style repentance was inauthentic. And so I
scrounged a ride from a German couple who were going to
vacation in a trullo with their three dogs, who were curled
up beside me on the back seat.

"Ever been to Puglia?" they asked me.

"Yeah, I love it."

Back in Rome, I found Za with his new girlfriend chosen
by God. I took it really hard.

My father made me get vaccinated for rabies because of
my car ride with the dogs.

I spent more sleepless nights mourning a future I had
opted out of. The tall guy continued to write to me, threatening to drive down to Rome in his convertible.

With Cecilia and Milena, I moved into the home of my grandma and grandpa, who'd both died by then. Theoretically we were supposed to make me get over my heartache by throwing parties every night, but basically I spent weeks crying, wearing a sweatsuit that I put on my first day there and never took off. Cecilia stayed on the sofa watching reruns of *Tatort*, beside her a frying pan that she was using as both a plate and an ashtray thanks to a wooden spoon acting as a divider. I didn't leave my grandpa's bed, and thought back on how happy I'd once been in it. Maybe I should never have left it. Milena stared at us with loathing and pity, did the shopping, bought us cigarettes, and went to answer the phone whenever it rang.

"If it's Za, tell him I don't want to talk to him."

"Don't worry, it's Francesca."

I went a month without stepping foot outside the house.

"Please, Vero, could you at least change out of that sweatsuit?" Milena begged me. "It's making me sick."

Since I'd stopped eating, the sweatsuit began to sag around my waist and I kept it up with a pair of my grandpa's suspenders. On my feet I wore his handmade leather slippers.

Za had set off with the girlfriend chosen by God for World Youth Day. Milena showed me a newscast about it, hoping to cheer me up. My jealousy took a turn for the surreal. Suddenly I wasn't suffering from the thought of them possibly screwing (how did that work for a new convert?) but of them blissfully singing songs of worship amid a throng of Papaboys, with Za on the guitar.

It was my aunt—my father's sister—who called an end to the torment. One day she showed up unannounced. She came in, walked around the apartment, then planted herself by the door and looked at me with her implacable blue eyes, identical to my grandpa's.

"You've disappointed me," she said. "I thought you were an artist." It wasn't the first time she'd brought up that stuff about me being an artist. When I was ten and painted my nails purple, she looked at my hands and said, "You've disappointed me. I thought you were an artist, not a dime-store cashier."

I was sorry she was disappointed, but it's not easy to know how to react if someone accuses you of not being an artist when you've never thought you were one to begin with.

"You know the state of things?" she asked sternly, standing in my grandparents' front doorway.

My aunt's questions are generally nonsensical enigmas, limericks that end with a question mark, but in this case Cecilia took a wild guess from the sofa: "*Der Stand der Dinge*, Wim Wenders, 1982."

"No, no," I said, "that's not what she means . . ."

"Yes it is," my aunt said.

It was because of Wim Wenders—whatever he was trying to tell us—that all three of us were kicked out of the house.

I objected to the eviction in a style that was perhaps a bit too colorful.

"It's so disappointing, all this foul language," my aunt said. "I thought you were—"

"Aw, fucking hell," I said. "I don't want to be an artist."

Years later I found out from a mutual friend that Za was getting married the following week. To a different chick. She too had been presented to him by God. Naturally I hadn't been invited to the wedding, but it seemed wrong not to even get in touch with him.

I called him two days before the wedding. He answered, his voice funereal.

"What the fuck, Za! Wow, you're getting married!"

"Oh, so you haven't heard?"

The mutual friend who'd told me about the wedding never bothered to tell me that right after that, Za had decided to call it off.

I'd been prepared for an embarrassing phone call, but not for *that* embarrassing phone call. I started to say goodbye.

"No, wait," he said. "I've been meaning to call you."

"You have?"

"Yeah. I dreamed about you."

As a rule I never believe it when people say they've dreamed about me, though to be polite I put up with listening to a recap of the dream and even its possible interpretation, but under those circumstances it seemed ridiculous that he would lie to me about it.

Not only had Za dreamed about me, but my apparition in the dream was what made him call off the wedding.

I still found myself dreaming about him, especially day-dreaming about him, when I used our past encounters as tried and tested material to masturbate to. Over time I'd elaborated a particular fantasy: he was this really shady guy who did filthy things to me, taking advantage of my conviction that I was a virgin. Even now, when I'm really out of ideas I might just dust off the character. I would gladly have told him about it if he hadn't started telling me about his dream first.

"I was in a long hallway," he said, "and at the end of the hallway was someone with their back to me."

"Naked?"

"No, very much dressed."

In Za's dream, he walked toward the "very much dressed" person until he realized it was a nun. The nun turned around and it was me. Actually, to be precise, the nun turned her head around 180 degrees. At that point my oneiric presence, in the nun-and-little-girl-from-*The-Exorcist* version, nodded to him, and he understood everything.

"And then?"

"And that's it."

"You mean, nothing filthy?"

"No. You were a nun."

"Exactly."

When Za actually did finally get married to the third girlfriend presented to him by God—by then his well-established public relations guy—I avoided getting in touch.

In my family we all used swear words. All of us except my mother, who endured them like the secondhand smoke from the two and a half soft packs of MS cigarettes my father smoked every day. My brother and I had picked up swear words when we were little. They didn't enter our vocabulary as something sordid and transgressive—quite the opposite. They were part of the ABC's of ordinary communication. Not only in the days of our potty training did we announce we had to "go piss" or "take a shit," but we also spared each other all the euphemisms. The first time a boy told me to shove it, I stared at him, confused. "Shove what?"

"It. Up your ass."

"Oh, okay."

During our long afternoons of boredom, my brother and I would calmly remark that we were "bored off our asses" or "bored off our tits," depending on our mood. None of us ever blasphemed (unlike nonno Peppino, who was crazy about blaspheming). I don't know if it was out of respect for the Lord or for some other reason. In any case, we weren't as sensitive to sexist implications when we had to swear, opting for "son of a bitch," "son of a whore," or "son of a harlot in heat," which was my father's favorite (strangely, he preferred the word "harlot" to "whore").

I was a pathologically shy girl. I bottled up all the anger that in years to come would keep me awake at night, but on the rare occasions I uttered anything to others, I might happen to throw in a vulgarity, which usually caused a sense of bewilderment in my interlocutor. Most times they figured they'd misunderstood, since I barely spoke loud enough to be heard. Fortunately this spared both of us the embarrassment of my having to repeat myself.

But one day, in first grade, back when most of my class-mates could barely even write the alphabet, my teacher forced me to fill two pages with the sentence "*I will not call the janitor a dipshit.*" I don't remember whether there were quotation marks around the word "dipshit."

I'd called him that because while I was walking back from the bathroom he pretended he was going to trip me, pulling his foot back at the last minute with a sly smile. Back then, my insults weren't randomly uttered swear words, but part of a well-mannered formula: "I'm sorry, but don't you think that's a dipshit move?" Once, at the supermarket, I gently tapped the arm of a man who'd been standing in front of a shelf for ten minutes. "Excuse me, would you mind getting out of my fucking way?"

Anyway, I never would've imagined the janitor would go tell my teacher, though sharing their resentment toward all children was their favorite pastime. I've never understood why they ended up in their line of work—they viewed it like a case of bad karma. The janitor wanted to be a soccer player and my teacher was a ballerina. At some point their bodies must have betrayed them, and I think in the spring in every step of our youthful bodies they glimpsed the shadow of that betrayal.

My teacher still had the posture of a ballerina. She was petite and always perfectly straight-backed, like a bishop on a chessboard, and she wished we children would follow her example and do nothing else in life: stay upright, in our place, on the chessboard.

Telling me I had to fill two pages was actually an empty threat, one of those purely conceptual postures meant to reestablish discipline, because she didn't really expect I'd actually be able to do it. Instead, I was perfectly happy to set myself apart from the rest of the class and concentrate, my head bowed over the assignment ("*I will not call the janitor a dipshit.*" I wrote the first page in cursive and the second in print). My classmates looked over my shoulder to behold the wonder. Then the teacher also came over, visibly moved. And it was the first time someone finally told me "Brava!" for knowing how to write.

When the teacher took the pages to the janitor, he too was moved, and from then on when he saw me he always respectfully raised a hand to his forehead: "Signor Dipshit salutes you." I would reply with my mumbled hello, red in the face.

My mother is convinced my brother and I have never become successful writers because we use too many swear words. She sees our vice as an act of self-sabotage, but in it she also sees the last glimmers of our youthful rebellion toward her. There's not one thing she doesn't take personally. Every year she threatens to give us a diction course for Christmas.

"Sorry, Mamma, but what the fuck does a diction course have to do with anything?"

When she hears some writer being interviewed on Radio 3, she's not the least bit interested in what they say, just in how they say it: "Well, you can tell he's smart, but he's still got a *terrone* accent." Her Apulian origins protect her from being accused of racism, maybe a bit like when Black people call each other the N-word. Even when she's watching a movie and isn't focusing on taking inspiration from the furniture in the characters' homes to decorate the one she'll never buy, she's focusing on the actors' diction.

"Robert Redford speaks so well!"

"What the fuck, Mamma, it's dubbed."

"For Christmas, what if I gave you two a dubbing course?"

My vulgar language also caused problems when I went to Cecilia's. Her father was a stern, distinguished, imposing man, the son of industrialists from the North. Though he never missed his chance to intimate that he'd been particularly active in the years of armed struggle in the seventies and eighties, enjoying the astonished look on my face when his stories suddenly mentioned guns or kneecappings, he wasn't as indulgent when it came to another kind of violence: foul language.

His four daughters, who were all very tall, had equestrian postures, played the piano, never rested their elbows on the dinner table, and never used colorful language. He'd have had no problem with them going out at night to kill Fascists, but good manners came first and foremost.

When I couldn't hold back a "fucking hell" after the story of a successful ambush followed by a thrashing, he gently tapped his pipe twice and looked at me seriously: "Please, we're not at the stadium" (where he'd never been, mind you, given that soccer was the new opium of the people).

I envied Glenda her mother's easygoing attitude and Cecilia her father's class. She had absorbed that classiness, adapting it to her youthful body, and she was the only person I've ever known who was capable of literally pissing herself laughing, turning that particular form of incontinence into something endearing. I've seen her piss herself a dozen times with all those present being charmed and daunted by the radical gesture.

During college, Cecilia and I set off together for a summer in Mexico.

By the end of the trip we were both crippled from dysentery, but my ticket back was for the day before hers. She came with me to the airport and when the woman at the ticket counter refused to change her flight, Cecilia threatened to defecate in front of everyone. I smiled at the provocation, but didn't realize how serious she was.

"Okay, here I go," she said, dumping her backpack next to the counter and going to the center of the hall with her regal stride. Surrounded by the crowds of Mexicans, she looked even taller. Inaccessible. Monumental. She squatted, keeping her back perfectly straight.

The woman at the counter and I exchanged a look of shocked admiration.

And that was how we managed to come back on the same flight.

When we landed at Fiumicino several hours later, I couldn't find one of my boots. I'd taken them off and one had dematerialized during the flight. We stayed on board while all the other passengers got off the plane, then searched for it with the flight attendants: beneath the seats, in the overhead compartments, in the bathroom, everywhere. There was no trace of it. To compensate, Cecilia found an Adidas sweatshirt and I found a carton of cigarettes. Then we both spotted a Swatch, but to avoid fighting over it, we left it with the airline.

My father came to pick us up in the car and didn't notice I was half-barefoot. I got out of the car and went upstairs, and finally my mother noticed I'd lost at least five kilos and one boot.

"We've reached the height of paradox," my father said.

He put a pot of water on to boil and emptied two bottles of rubbing alcohol into it. Then he poured it all into a basin.

I spent the night lying in bed with my foot immersed in the magic potion.

To afford our trip to Mexico, Cecilia and I had to work hard.

At first we began to knit woolen scarves and hats with the intention of hawking them on the street. After one week we'd made around one-fourth of a scarf, which looked more like a fishing net, so we were forced to come up with a more sophisticated plan.

We started ransacking every market stand we could find that sold used clothes, searching for handmade scarves, hats, and mittens. Each piece might have gone for at most five hundred to two thousand liras, with the occasional splurge

for a shawl at three thousand liras. Cecilia drew our logo—
two stylized hippies—and copied it onto a series of little
cardboard tags that she attached, using ecru cotton yarn, to
our precious pieces of handcraftsmanship, which we would
sell with a markup of two thousand percent.

To avoid being caught off guard if a potential customer
pestered us with questions about our creations, we studied
The Complete Guide to Knitting Techniques from cover to
cover, but it turns out that people who bought handmade
scarves without realizing they'd been picked out of a pile of
old rags and rejuvenated with lots of Perlana fabric softener
and some bespoke packaging generally didn't have a particularly in-depth understanding of the subtleties of knitwear.

We also found that people thought our logo with the two
stylized hippies was adorable, so we started dressing like
them. We'd leave our apartments in the outskirts of town
decked out like the flower children seen in advertisements, in
bell-bottoms or long skirts with immaculate hems, colorful
blousy tops, straight combed-out hair with a part down the
middle, and ribbons tied around our necks. We set up our
little stand on the sidewalks downtown, near the Pantheon
or in Piazza Navona, where the street musicians played. The
traffic cops patrolling the area came to like having us around,
and when they went to get coffee at the café, they'd even bring
some back to us along with a *bignè alla crema*.

"You two remind me of my daughter," one of them said, with a surge of affection that in seconds turned into paternal anguish. But his daughter, he reassured us, was at home studying for the exam to join the city police force.

During Christmas break we managed to rake in over a hundred thousand liras a day. One afternoon a director hired us as extras in his movie, to play the part we were already playing: two hippies selling scarves on the street. Still, the part brought in another hundred thousand liras we hadn't been expecting.

My parents were oblivious to my entrepreneurial activities, even though I sold a hat to a colleague of my mother's, who didn't recognize me and wanted to commission an identical hat for a friend of hers (who knows, maybe for my mother).

Luckily, Cecilia was quick on her feet. "No, sorry, we only make one-of-a-kind items," she said.

"Well, what if it was in a different color?"

"No, out of the question," Cecilia said with the resentment of an offended artist. "It's a matter of inspiration."

Anyway, when my mother saw me leaving the house dressed up like a hippie she was strangely euphoric. "Oh, how it reminds me of when I was young," she said, though her experience as a flower child had been even faker than mine, and amounted to nothing more than some photos taken in student housing where she was pretending to play the guitar and smoke a bidi.

On the other hand, when Cecilia's father found out about our business, he had nothing against the scam, but he was particularly upset that we'd been fraternizing with the cops.

When we ran out of merchandise, we went back out onto the streets with only our bodies. If we could pass ourselves off as skilled knitters, we might as well pass ourselves off as two simple runaways. At that point we moved our business to Trastevere. Pretending the streets of the more bohemian district were our 1960s San Francisco seemed more reasonable.

"*Help us get to Mexico,*" we wrote on a sign.

Incredibly, people helped us. I don't know why. What drove them to support the cause of two university girls who wanted to take a trip to Mexico? Or maybe precisely that—our lack of any real need, our artificial form of destitution, and the feasibility of our plan—is what struck them as reassuring. Maybe it was easier to accept a fleeting thanks than eternal gratitude. In any case, we never went so far as to reach out our hands to beg for money, as though the gesture would be the ultimate sign of encroachment, of trespassing into a territory we weren't sure we wanted to enter. We let people drop their change into a straw hat that was supposed to represent a sombrero.

Thinking back on it today, I don't know what's stronger, my nostalgia for that bravery—sitting there on the ground begging for change—or my sense of guilt over swindling people.

The feeling is likely yet another, the awareness that I didn't do the one thing that would've given new meaning to my present life: becoming what I was pretending to be. Agreeing to reach out my hand, cutting ties with my family, setting off for Mexico, setting off for anywhere, living "on the road," disappearing.

The money we made selling fake handicrafts helped us pay for the plane tickets, but once in Mexico, Cecilia and I were supposed to be earning room and board by working for the theater festival in Morelia through one of those nonprofit organizations that were all the rage back then, the ones that let Western youths pick potatoes and corn or shear sheep somewhere in the world, adding an exotic touch to the "*Other Experience*" section of their résumés. Cecilia had scoured all the field work destinations and found among the long list of rural activities the dream job of working for a theater festival. No skills were required, just goodwill.

Once we got to Morelia, we discovered that cosmic justice does its duty and that if you use fraud to get yourself to Mexico, you risk ending up defrauded. There was no festival. There was no board. And the room was a single dorm where we were expected to sleep with six other girls who were just as lacking in skills and full of goodwill. At the head of this Dadaist volunteer experiment was Jenny, a tall, burly Californian girl with blond hair and a fair complexion.

Jenny didn't seem at all fazed by the misunderstanding. In fact, the need to improvise made her eyes sparkle and her teeth gleam. She sat us down on the floor in the middle of the room—then again, there were no chairs—and proposed her new plan. A "project" with the local juvenile correctional facility. A male one.

"What project?" I asked.

"Let's find out together!" Jenny said.

We were eight twenty-year-olds with suitcases full of ripped jeans and sundresses who were capable of traveling the world to put together nonexistent theater festivals, and Jenny was convinced that Mexican teens who'd been locked up for stealing a chicken might be interested in hearing about our life stories, not to mention that all this would need to be done through telepathy, given that, with the exception of Cecilia, none of us spoke a single word of Spanish. But who cared!

One of the eight of us, another American girl, stood up to say she could teach funky dance. She did a few moves to show us she knew her stuff. There was applause. Jenny was enthusiastic. Then she asked Cecilia and me, "What can you do?"

That question has never—not before or since then—been asked of me point-blank like that, and I found myself wandering a void of words, lost, naked, facing an unknown that will stay with me until the day I die. But Jenny, genetically incapable of handling silence for more than a few seconds, took a stab for us: "Want to teach them how to make pizza?"

The next morning, before dawn, Cecilia and I snuck out and caught a bus to Mexico City.

But that day Jenny had to deal with a problem even more unpleasant than the clandestine escape of two volunteers. The dorm room in the farmhouse we'd been staying in was spared the primordial trill, since it had no phone, but the same couldn't be said of the single room where Jenny had hoped to sleep in peaceful isolation. My mother has never quite grasped the concept of time zones. To her it seems like pointless sophistry with no scientific basis.

"Hello! Hello! Here Francesca! Mother of Verika."

I imagine Jenny at six a.m. rushing into the dorm room in her pajamas, still half asleep, to announce that Francesca's on the phone. I imagine her plunging into a state of horror at the sight of the two empty bunks. I imagine her making flimsy reassurances when threatened with reports being filed with Interpol. I imagine that scorching-hot morning dragging into afternoon and then into nightfall, with her crumpled on the floor, receiver in hand, enduring the interminable hours with the fear she's lost everything: her job, her enthusiasm, her faith in funky dance.

That night I called my mother from a phone booth near the hostel in Mexico City, pretending to be in Morelia, but by then Jenny had become her best friend.

"Was making a pizza too much to ask?"

Despite all this, for years I left "*Organizer of the Morelia Theater Festival*" in the "*Other Experience*" section of my résumé.

"Dear Jenny," I'd like to say to her now, "I don't know how to make pizza and, though I'm sure my mother tried to convince you otherwise, it's not true that I know how to draw. Anyway, who says having a talent is better than not having one? If you asked me now what I can do, I'd sink into the same embarrassed state I did when I was twenty, but if there's one thing I've learned since then, it's that I fear the truth more than death."

A while back I sent the first part of this book to my brother. He replied with one touching message and another in which he told me he'd had his girlfriend read it, and she thought it was funny.

I didn't know whether to feel flattered or irritated, but out of that minimum principle of sisterhood I thought that if I was in his girlfriend's shoes, I'd be happy to find out sooner than later what kind of family I'd be dealing with in the years to come.

Then, a couple weeks later, he announced he was writing a novel about our family. I took it badly.

It's impossible to argue with my brother, because he never sees what the problem is.

"We can't both write a book about our family."

"Why not?"

There was no answer to his "Why not?" if not a childish "Because I said so."

I envied siblings who argued over an inheritance, over a house. It seemed like a more dignified affair. When all was said and done, one of the contenders would get something out of it.

I regressed in my reasoning. "It's no fair. I started mine first."

He regressed in his. "Hey, I know you were lying about rolling all those fives."

We'd reached an aporia, so he seized his chance. "Well, ever heard the parable of the budding fig tree?"

Up until that moment, the fact that we were both writers had turned out to be mutually beneficial. Not that we gave each other moral support, but we were accomplices engaged in constant trafficking. Over the years we'd farmed out jobs to each other: articles, reviews, prefaces, postscripts, a writer's viewpoint on the comeback of leggings or the end of literature, even entire short stories and highly inspired verses. Our price list changed depending on how much money we had at the time or how anxious we were to finish, and even verged on the extortionate during emergencies.

"I need to turn it in tomorrow morning."

"Okay."

"I'm missing three thousand characters."

"Make me an offer."

The first few times we still had some semblance of ethics, or maybe just simple paranoia. We left each other time to tweak things, to nitpick. We rearranged what the other gave us in a more personal style. For example, I changed his "whilst" into "while."

Gradually even this form of caution disappeared. If people read our writings and didn't notice the scam, it's not because our styles were similar or because we were skilled chameleons, but because deep down nobody gave a damn. In a way it was therapeutic, a form of depersonalization, diminishment of the ego. We could go on cultivating our narcissism as writers, but we had proof that it was all an illusion.

Taking a more subversive view, we could convince ourselves we'd mastered the flaws of the system. Cognitive precariat, brainworkers: were we all really interchangeable? Fine, we would use the extortion of the cultural market as a weapon against itself. We would become counterfeiters. In our minds we devised conceptual manifestos: "The author is dead! No, wait: he's alive, and he's his sister!"

But to be completely honest, the market was sleeping peacefully while we had to grapple with pangs of conscience.

The only time I've ever actually been a sellout, I used my brother's work. My latest novel was about to be published, and one morning my editor called me, sounding excited.

"I've got crazy good news for you!"

Did they want to turn my novel into a movie? Had they already sold translation rights in thirty countries?

No. The "crazy"—this being an adjective my editor loves—good news is that I was being given the opportunity to write for a newspaper, reviewing the unpublished manuscript of a famous author whose book was coming out through the same publisher shortly before mine.

The market wanted to give me a little lesson in trafficking.

I wanted to say no. Which is in fact what I did.

"Sorry, it's too late," my editor said with unwavering enthusiasm.

The bound galleys were delivered to my place while we were still talking on the phone.

"Can I at least write what I really think about it?"

"No."

"Can I suggest it between the lines?"

"No."

"Add a couple *mehs*?"

"Meh."

"No?"

"No."

They'd given me an entire double-page spread. It was the longest article of my career and I'd never written for that particular newspaper before. Obviously no one had brought up the question of money, and I didn't have my mother there beside me to bring it up herself.

I started reading the manuscript, then called my brother in tears.

He sensed his bargaining power. "Let's make it five hundred."

"Chri, five hundred euros! Are you kidding?"

"Take it or leave it."

I accepted.

What I turned in was the piece my brother wrote. The people from the paper called to compliment my work. "It's good, great. This is the beginning of a long collaboration."

I never heard from them again. I never wrote for that paper again. But most importantly I was never paid for it, unlike my brother.

The one good thing is that my shame over being a sellout has kept me from doing it again.

I've also wondered whether I could consider it an aggravating or attenuating circumstance, the fact that my brother wrote it. How to measure the degree of individual responsibility? And what is it exactly that defines being a sellout? If it's unpaid, does it become less ignoble? I, however, had ventured even further, had partly subverted its nature: I'd paid money out of my own pocket for it. I asked myself: if a prostitute pays the customer, is she still a prostitute? No, that wasn't even it, because I hadn't paid the customer. The situation was actually this: a prostitute blindfolds the customer and pays another prostitute to screw him in her place. Then which of the two is more embroiled?

There's more to the story. Later on, when I happened to meet the writer in question, she didn't have the slightest idea who I was. I didn't know if she was faking it, if she was doing it on purpose, if it was some sort of sick little game, a form of revenge, but then again, what for?

I promptly reintroduced myself, clearly pronouncing my first and last name as she shook my hand, her big eyes open wide, as though overcome by a sudden wave of tenderness at the sight of a panda. "So tell me," she said, "what do you do for a living?"

The last time I ran into her, I introduced myself as Ursula Le Guin.

She gave me the same look of tender surprise. "What an unusual name. So tell me, what do you do for a living?"

I've never written as many letters as the ones I wrote to Cecilia. Her letters back to me are still stored in a big box at my parents' place. One afternoon many years ago my mother decided to straighten out my correspondence, sorting it by topic. She even distinguished between "happy love letters," "sad love letters," and "pornographic love letters." She couldn't keep herself from circling in red the extra *m* where a classmate in middle school wrote to me, "*I often immagine your smile.*"

Since she put so much effort into it, the box has remained at her place, buried somewhere in the huge mass grave of the overhead storage space.

Cecilia and I wrote notes to each other while in class, while doing homework, in the sadness of our evenings as teens.

At some point, for fun, we started burying our letters beneath a big rock in the park in our neighborhood. I would go out, telling my folks I was going to the *gelateria* (the official alibi when I wanted to do something shady, whether it was running away from home or digging up letters with passages from Kundera and De Beauvoir).

We gave ourselves fake identities, nicknames that made us unidentifiable if someone ever lifted the rock and found

the envelope with our letters, though deep down we always
hoped a stranger would take a burning interest in our correspondence, thickening the plot.

As early as our first year of high school, Cecilia already had
splendidly illegible handwriting. Even in this I felt inferior
to her, with my lettering that was no longer childish but was
nevertheless scrupulously written. I hadn't yet freed myself
from a certain roundness, still felt it necessary to distinguish
the body of an *a* from that of an *e*, to dot every *i*. In Cecilia's
handwriting there were only vertical marks and horizontal
marks. It was impossible, for example, to tell whether a letter
was an *f* or an *l* or a *t*. All that work deciphering it made me
delve more deeply into her world. I reread words ten times,
went back over entire paragraphs. I enjoyed feeling like an
exegete of her writings.

I have occasionally copied down some of her sentences in
a notebook and reused them later to impress a person. I've
also reused the same sentence to impress more than one person. I prepared my compendium on amatory seduction and
over the following years casually honed my recycling skills.
I've plundered and plagiarized letters from old love stories
to express new passions until I lost track of the genealogy of
my most heartfelt lines. Until I convinced myself that such
genealogy wasn't important after all.

Cecilia spent her senior year of high school in Germany
as part of an academic mobility program. She went to live

with a family in a town near Dresden. Back then, people left Italy to go to London, but I didn't know anyone besides her who deliberately chose to learn German and spend a year of their life in some anonymous little town in the former GDR.

Naturally the number of letters we wrote to each other spiked.

Finally I could experience the thrill of finding them in the mailbox, complete with foreign postage. Sometimes she would attach snapshots: her two host brothers (blond, skinny, eight and twelve years old), who, like in the finest melodramas, were both in love with her, discovering in one fell swoop sibling rivalry, platonic love, and the fear of abandonment; a 1930s edition of *Der Zauberberg* she was reading in the original language; her first attempt at making lebkuchen; her in the snow wearing a hitchhiker's sheepskin jacket and leather pants à la Jim Morrison ("*My friend, I found them!*").

It was a search we'd begun together, a rite of initiation *in absentia*, considering there had been no initiation and that all our Sunday expeditions to the Porta Portese open market chasing after the mirage of a pair of leather pants à la Jim Morrison did nothing but confirm the solidity of our ideals at the expense of reality. But then she actually found them in that little town in the former GDR and sent me the proof. It was a blow to my values system: the moment an ideal materializes, theoretically it ceases to exist. Cecilia was living in the aftermath of Communism incarnate and was wearing the leather pants incarnate. I couldn't figure out whether it should make my confidence soar or cast me into the depths of despair.

Aside from their contents, the photographs themselves came from another world, as if her memories had to be stored in a different format to evoke their sense of belonging. The size was smaller and the matte finish blurred the colors. In them was the intrinsic melancholy of Eastern Europe. To me, its exoticism lay in the images: white sky, big buildings, small windows, and playgrounds with wooden equipment.

Our physical distance also had another effect. The fake names we'd given each other to make ourselves unidentifiable in the eyes of others had already caused a certain distancing from ourselves, a first mechanism in autofiction. Now there was a new phenomenon to that distance: we could make shit up. I don't know if she did, but I sure did.

There are at least two versions of my senior year of high school: the more or less real one, of which I remember almost nothing, and the one I wrote about to Cecilia, of which I remember almost everything. In a certain way, it was my first novel.

Almost ten years later, when I found out I was actually going to publish a novel, Cecilia had moved to Palma de Mallorca with her comic-book-artist boyfriend, was getting a PhD in theater, and taught German. She read the galleys of the book and wrote to me this:

Let's hope, I told myself, let's hope it doesn't talk
about, doesn't describe anyplace in Rome, any
high school, that it doesn't quote twenty-five other
writers, that it isn't pleased with the decline of
the landscape, that there isn't even one party, one
province, that it's full of anger and love, love that's
actually made and not sublimated, like in that
book by ***. I was really scared, Vero, as though
of a betrayal. I feel a bit foolish now, but basically
relieved. I can't help but think of Rome, of that
environment, which—I know, it's a bit immature
to think about it from here and still "as much as I
love it"—is so highly contaminative (and under-
going tribal cannibalism).

With time, *** and I have ended up hanging out, and we
often talk about books, now that I'm no longer able to find
either anger or love in them. *** can, or at least claims to
be able to, though nevertheless while speaking of love, passionately, as a substantive topic (right after sex and mothers,
though, so maybe it's still a matter of sublimation). On the
other hand, I don't see Cecilia anymore. Haven't for years.
The two things are entirely unrelated, though somehow I
wish there was a connection. I wish anything had a connection to Cecilia's disappearance from my life, because I don't
know how to explain it.

She still lives in Palma, where I've never gone to visit her, and she has a daughter I've never met. There have been her sisters' weddings, other children, other events I haven't been there for. To tell the truth, there are a bunch of kids for whom I've never cut out a role for myself as a godmother, aunt, stepsister, babysitter, or simple acquaintance. Basically they're born and I vanish. *Poof!* Like a fairy in a vocational crisis. I can get choked up over the birth of a baby hedgehog, a baby fox or bear cub; when I'm upset, I soothe myself by watching videos of little owls making funny calls, but the moment I see a human baby come into the world and hear it wail, I don't know what to do. I just nod. Okay, I say. And that's it. I say okay and I disappear. All the same, I'm invited to their birthdays, and theoretically I'd be off to a head start: I wouldn't even have to spend any money to get them baby clothes, given my stockpile of all the ones my mother has bought for her imaginary grandchildren.

"And this is your zia Vero. Say hello to zia Vero." The infant in question does nothing, because they know I'm not their aunt and they owe me nothing, and I too do nothing, because I continue not to know what it is I should be doing, no matter how much I search inside myself for all the affection I've felt toward the little tiger cub recently born at the zoo in some European capital.

Gradually I've stopped getting even those invitations, and my disappearance is now complete.

My mother likes to run down the list of my girlfriends' procreative lives, but today I couldn't say how many children they have or their ages. To me, this indeterminate time boils down to "a couple years." If I can't remember when something happened I say "a couple years ago," and if I don't know a child's age I decide they must be "two years old, more or less." My world is populated by two-year-old creatures, gender unknown, who I hope will one day become adults, but until that day they'll remain shrouded in a haze of uncertainty.

The only time I've ever felt a maternal instinct was one Christmas in Berlin. It was the first Christmas I'd ever spent without my family, and though I was the one who came up with the excuse that there were no more available flights back to Italy, that morning I woke up to snow and raging homesickness. A friend of mine had told me about a party in a big building on the riverside. He'd given me the directions, a little hand-drawn map I'd studied in detail to kill my time spent alone. That night I wound up wandering the darkness through muddy slush and frozen puddles until I found an abandoned factory that matched his description. From the outside you couldn't hear music or voices from a party. I walked in, and though my friend wasn't there, there was a handful of young stoners warming themselves around an open fire with a charred suckling pig roasting over it. No one turned to look at me, no one seemed to notice me show up. Lying on the floor were sleeping children. I introduced myself, my name rising into the emptiness of the room and no one interested in catching it; I couldn't even entrench myself in the unpleasant sensation of feeling like an intruder, since the intrusion hadn't even registered. Sitting down with them around the fire, beneath the pig, I picked up a carton of red wine and poured some into a mug with ACAB written on it, a mug somebody had already drunk out of. The little group bobbed its head and continued to ignore me. I'd brought a bottle of spumante, but it seemed out of place to pop it open, and I didn't want to wake the children. Then I was gripped by an agonizing thought: the terror that those bundles on the floor were actually dead bodies. I went over to touch their wrists, one by one, and listen for their breathing. They weren't dead. One little girl opened her eyes and flashed me an incredible smile—or maybe it was an ordinary smile, but it was the first sign of life I'd seen since I'd shown up. She stared at me, looking more curious than surprised. Not knowing what to do, I started stroking her hair. It was blond, with little natural dreadlocks. She grabbed my elbow and told me, "I have to pee."

I took her by the hand and walked her outside. The temperature was below zero. She wore only a big flannel shirt and tights with holes in them, tucked into rubber boots. I took her over to some bushes and she squatted, gracefully lifting the hem of her shirt. From the ground rose a little cloud of steam that made her laugh. "We have to hide it," she told me as she stood up. You couldn't see anything, but we covered it all with leaves anyway. She stood there staring at the little pile, illuminated by my lighter. She seemed satisfied. I nodded to her, as if to say, "Yeah, we did a good job."

We went back inside. My invisibility made her invisible too, and in that disappearance from view, from the world, from Christmas toasts, in which we found ourselves together for a few hours one night, in the toxic air of a dying fire, it occurred to me that that was my idea of a family: a little girl and an older girl who didn't know each other and would never see each other again.

After long years of silence, Cecilia wrote to me six years ago because she was in Rome. My closest friends from high school had organized a reunion at ten in the morning at Villa Borghese. They'd all become parents. The plan was to meet up there with their strollers. It was a bitter cold day in February, but sunny. I rarely get out of bed before eleven, but that morning I was up at seven, staring at the blue of the winter sky. The thought of seeing Cecilia again had me anxious, filled me with emotion. The day before, I'd gone for my abortion. At five minutes after ten I texted her: "*Sorry. I can't.*"

And then another: "*I'll call you later to explain.*"

She didn't reply and I didn't call.

In my life I never see the glass half full. Or half empty. I always see it on the verge of toppling over. Or I don't see it at all. There is no glass. Nothing's there. I'm staring at an ugly table with nothing on it. The table itself might disappear. In fact, it already has. What I'm left with isn't its absence, only puzzlement.

Sorry, I can't remember. What is it I was supposed to see again?

I don't know where to find the answer, because at that point the question has also disappeared.

At times I wonder whether the constant uncertainty in which I live depends on one of my innate characteristics: no one ever recognizes me. Not just my relatives in Puglia, the author for whom I paid someone else to be a sellout, or people I met at a party and chatted with for only a few minutes, but even my closest friends.

There's a guy that wanders my neighborhood who asks you for a hug and then touches your ass. Even though I know what's going to happen, I let him do it, thinking of my frustration when I reach out to someone for a hug only to see them take a step back because they don't recognize me. There's always something that doesn't fit: I'm wearing sunglasses, my hair is shorter, longer, I dyed it, I'm wearing heels, I got a tan, my hood's up, I've got a scarf on, I'm eating a *supplì* and they can't see my mouth.

Once I auditioned for my friend who's a director. That night he called me in anguish after seeing the recording. "It was like watching a horror movie. You have no idea."

"No, I don't, actually."

He claimed I was literally changing faces in every shot.

I had the same problem during my years together with A. He's a photographer. If he were a woman he'd say he's an artist who uses a camera as a means of expression, but since he's a man he simply says he's a photographer. Unfortunately this didn't keep him from feeling like an artist whenever he had to take a picture of me.

I'm sorry for all those women who've suffered from being relegated to the role of mere muses in front of a camera lens, but I want to reassure them: it could've been much worse. A. was never interested in photographing me, there was always something more important in the world: a particular limestone formation, a cluster of rotting leaves, a crumbling wall. The few portraits I have were extorted from him or bartered for something else ("Okay, but then you have to write my project for the Biennale").

It was always a mystery to me, what he saw when he focused on my face, what happened in that space of air and light between the camera lens and the confines of my body, in the contemplative lull in which I begged him not to frame me from below and he was immersed in the silence of creation. All the same, the results were embarrassing pictures of my monstrified face. In the agonized deformations of my features, A. noticed the dark lines, shadows, visual stratifications: not the face of a beloved person, but a landscape that was unsettling, ruinous, like a revelatory ugliness that reared its head into the world and seemed to appease the artist within him.

"I'm horrendous."

"But it's a good picture."

He always said it in a way that was disarmingly frank, which made it even more painful. We were each afflicted with our own visual disability: he couldn't see me and I couldn't see his photo.

With my mother, it's another situation entirely. When I have plans to meet her, I show up only to find her affectionately kissing some random woman. If I'm lucky, she's at least picked one who's about the same age as me, though the rest is completely arbitrary: height, build, wardrobe. Once she was mortified because I'd gotten a tribal tattoo that covered my whole arm, another time she was scared out of her wits because I'd gotten a dog (nonna Muccia used to beat stray dogs and cats to death with her broom, and this, rather than driving my mother to become a WWF activist, instilled in her a phobia of animals).

Usually, though, the surrogate version of her daughter
satisfies her more than the real one does. She thinks I look
good with curly hair, finally I've put on a few kilos, or she
loves the white quilted down coat I bought myself. If I'm not
on time, her latest victim—after apologizing for not being
me—will nevertheless be forced to undergo my mother's
third degree. At that point my turning up does nothing
but ruin their wonderfully intimate conversation, and I'm
enthusiastically informed about the life of this surrogate
daughter, who's a mother, who has a proper employment
contract, or a caring husband who supports her, and a nice
home in some residential area of Rome, preferably with a
terrace, or at least a little balcony where she can hang out
her laundry. Finally, they exchange phone numbers and
invitations to lunch. Sometimes the surrogate daughter,
feeling uncomfortable, hazards a question about me, but
before I can answer, my mother provides her with a summary of my whole life story: "When she was little she liked
to draw. Then she stopped." On her phone, she shows the
woman the two paintings hanging in the hallway. The surrogate daughter nods, as do I.

My mother also tries to pick up surrogate daughters
online. She and I aren't friends on Facebook. In fact, to be
precise, I blocked her so she'd stay out of my business. I've
never told her I separated from A. and that I've been living
on my own for almost two years now, because I was afraid of

a spike in phone calls, and I didn't want her to figure it out by not recognizing the wall behind me during a Facebook Live event.

To compensate, she's friended a whole series of female writers. She calls to tell me about their day, about how they feel, about how they've decorated their home, about how they fare in the kitchen ("Would you look at these beautiful cookies?"), about what they've read, about their love lives ("I liked her last boyfriend more").

Above all she calls me when they post photos of their own mothers when they were young. She's always touched by the sight of those pictures. She sees a part of herself, something that seemed lost forever before reappearing in the emotional memory of a surrogate daughter. She feels seen by those eyes, loved by those eyes, by the tender thoughtfulness of those who sat down to sort through their family photos and choose a memory to share with the world. She loves all the hearts, the comments below: "*How wonderful . . .*", "*Great picture!!!!!!*", "*Beautiful, heart and soul.*" She was really struck by a woman captured on film in 1962 in a skiing outfit against a backdrop of the Swiss Alps. My mother has never been to the Alps, or to Switzerland, and has never even worn a pair of skis.

At that point, to be consistent, she goes searching through the writers' photo collections for pictures of them when they were little, as though leafing through my childhood album. Given that no such album has ever existed in my case and all

I'm left with are the pictures my grandpa took of my back, I realize the image of my face as a child is entirely artificial, fluid, nothing more than an idea, the nostalgic memory of a quiet eight-year-old who really liked to draw.

When I landed on the cover of a magazine along with four other female writers, I called my mother to surprise her. I told her to go to the newsstand and buy a copy.

"Does it come free with the newspaper?"

She wanted to be sure it was worth the two-euro investment, so before completing the transaction she called me from the newsstand, magazine in hand.

"Verika, I don't understand what it is I'm supposed to see."

"Mamma, what the fuck! The cover!"

At that point she complimented my fluffy hairdo, mistaking me for one of the other writers.

A while back, in Berlin, I saw a play that talked about missing bodies. Mothers of Argentinean desaparecidos, mothers from Central America searching for their children who'd disappeared while crossing through Mexico, Kurdish mothers protesting the PKK's abducting their children and forcibly conscripting them. The importance of having a body to embrace again or, worst-case scenario, to bury. A body to weep over. A body to return to. The despondent, devastated faces of these mothers who'd searched for a body for years and found themselves with nothing but its absence. Death is appalling, but the impossibility of mourning is inhumane.

I thought of my mother in the tragic event she had to identify my remains. I wouldn't want to be in her shoes. I thought of how lost she would feel. I thought of her face: it wasn't despondent, wasn't devastated. It was just really confused. What would she do? Would she search for an ask-the-audience lifeline in the eyes of the people around her? In those of my father, looking down on her from heaven? ("We've reached the height of paradox.") Would she weep over the curly-haired remains of a woman with big boobs who weighed twenty kilos more than her daughter? As I imagined my mother facing that impossible dilemma, all I wanted, with all my soul, was for her to get out of that predicament as quickly as possible.

"Oh, whatever. Let's just say this is her."

And that's how I've felt at every moment of my life: Oh, whatever. Let's just say this is me.

"Cecilia and I grew apart" is the simplest way to put something that can't be explained. And yet, inside me I feel I know the reasons why—or better, I'm afraid I know them, and then I think back on that line in her message: "*I was really scared, Vero, as though of a betrayal.*"

Did I betray her?

I never used to dream of becoming a writer, though I've got my lies about it down to a science: "Of course! A dream I've nurtured since I was a little girl."

Actresses have the privilege of being discovered on the street, at a bus stop, or as they're wiping down tables at a diner. Lucky breaks become their attitude, a pose they strike even on the red carpet, while a writer needs to feel the sacred fire burning within her as early as childhood. And so I continue the lie, and stoke the fire with little invented anecdotes, moments of despair, or demons that kept me awake at night to gift me a few obsessions.

Once I heard a writer say that in order to write, she'd be willing to die. I don't doubt her sincerity, but I don't understand how that's supposed to work. If someone is willing to die for their country, I imagine they're willing to perish in battle in its defense, but what does it mean, being willing to die in order to write? Unfortunately no one, not even I, asked her to give a practical example.

When I was little I wanted to become the rock star Veronika, then I wanted to become a farmer, and at some point, given the success of my stolen paintings, I even toyed with the idea of reinventing myself as an artist—at least my aunt would've been happy. I could imagine myself at the vernissage of my exhibit, but not at work on a painting. I wasn't particularly drawn to the creative moment (Where did you start? Did you buy a canvas? Make a sketch? Forever reject the figurative? Even here, there were demons that would torment the artist, but they always left me alone). I liked the idea of having an atelier, and that was that.

As for being a rock star, I've never learned to play anything, and in general when I start singing, people always ask me to stop, which makes me kind of sad. My mother insisted that my brother and I learn to play the piano, because she thought a piano seemed like something nice to own, even though I wanted to play the bass guitar.

One day, at our place there arrived a white piano that was completely out of tune and was missing keys, a gift from her colleague Pariani, the music teacher. It was plunked down in the living room, and when you went to sit on the sofa you would always bang into it. My father invariably cursed at this new form of paradox, though this time I agreed with him.

Given that my mother had a soft spot for Pariani, she took on the burden of the piano so he would come to our place to give us lessons. Neither my brother nor I was particularly gifted, but most importantly, my mother had no intention of having the piano fixed. She just couldn't see the point.

"It's enough if they learn to pick out a tune," she said.

"Francesca, even to pick out a tune you need a piano with keys."

"Then pretend."

And so for a while Pariani taught us to pretend to pick out a tune.

The torture ended, for both us and Pariani, the day my father decided to dismember the piano and use the back of it to build a new partition wall. To compensate, Veronika was an awesome bass guitarist.

I've never had an image of myself in the future that wasn't entirely a pipe dream. Pipe dreams usually help us fool ourselves, whereas I wanted to fool others. I didn't think I had undiscovered talent, didn't feel misunderstood, didn't harbor any need to prove myself with a vengeance. Instead, it was like believing in the stars, in the Absolute, in the supremacy of five, magical thinking, a superstition like any other. I've always had fake, superficial ambition. Cultivating a dream, in the long term, is as boring as cultivating a

vegetable garden. In fact, even the idea of being a farmer
was kind of false, because all that interested me was looking out at my field with a hat on my head, the apple and
cherry trees in bloom, and a farmhouse always full of baby
animals, bonsai creatures forever prevented from growing
into adults.

When Cecilia and I talked about books, the truth is we
were never talking about books. They didn't exist as objects.
There were stories, characters, and naturally there was also
someone who'd written them and who had just as novelesque
a life, but there were no publishers, editors, proofreaders,
distributors, not to mention press offices. Basically, there
was no environment that was *so highly contaminative (and
undergoing tribal cannibalism)."* Then I found myself in the
midst of it. I too had been contaminated.

It would make things easier for me to think that between
Cecilia and me, she should've been the one to end up writing.
That kind of explanation would help justify my discomfort,
even literary, at feeling I had succumbed to an unexpressed
phantom.

Instead, what I miss are my afternoons digging up letters
in the park, or my afternoons in senior year when, since
Cecilia was gone, I started talking to Amory Blaine, the main
character in Fitzgerald's *This Side of Paradise*.

Amory used to wait for me every day at the school gates to walk me home. There was clearly an attraction between us. He was always well dressed, in a close-fitting dress suit and a silk ruffled shirt. Cuff links at his wrists. I tried to get rid of any potential company so I could be alone with him. I could feel his mocking gaze on my back as he leaned against the school wall, waiting for me to finish my little charade of coming up with excuses. Then I would go over to him and we would walk off together in silence, if not for our sighs.

"Is your mother home?" he asked me.

"Oh, Amory . . ." and I blushed.

He lit a cigarette.

"Amory, don't smoke. You'll stunt your growth."

"I don't care," he said gloomily.

But obviously I loved seeing him all gloomy, a cigarette in his mouth.

We walked down the porticoes of my building from stairway Q to reach mine, stairway A. We stopped in the foyer.

"Why on earth are we here?" he said.

"I don't know. I'm just full of the devil."

"Let's be frank . . . We'll never see each other again. I wanted to come out here with you because I thought you were the best-looking girl in sight."

And at that point, devastated but flattered, I rushed up the stairs to break up the peaceful moment between my mother and brother, who had already settled down to watch *Non è la RAI* with a cordon bleu on their plates.

A few years ago, during my summers in Berlin, I started hanging out at a bar simply because I had fallen for the bartender. He was twenty, Irish, and his name was Art. He reminded me of Amory, but maybe he reminded me of the person I no longer was. I went there almost every day and pretended to write. Actually, he too pretended to work, given that he spent all his time reading unknown Irish poets behind the bar, and then would come over to recite them to me. If I asked for a glass of wine, he finished the rest of the bottle. So as not to pollute the aesthetic orthodoxy of those afternoons with Art, I didn't bring my computer with me, and would scribble down lines in a notebook. He had the good manners not to ask how old I was (thirty-eight). I played along with his belief—at least, that was my illusion—that I was much younger than I actually was.

He called himself a poet, and though he read verses of poets who'd obviously been published, given that he was holding their books in his hand, he lived dreaming of a life spent wandering the world as a drunkard and pariah, and was horrified by the idea that one day he might end up signing a contract and seeing his poetry printed on a product with a bar code. I read him poems—translated there on the spot—that I'd written when I was fifteen, and we enjoyed that life which came before any decisions, before any debuts, before any of the marketing department's skepticism about the cover. But one day he had the terrible idea of googling my name and discovered I'd already published two novels. The intimacy of those afternoons suddenly became useless. He started ignoring me.

"Look, I barely sold any copies," I said, trying to reassure him.

He stopped reciting verses to me and started finishing bottles all on his own.

Then he moved to Greece, and today he too has a son. (Must be two years old, more or less.) I stare at his pictures on Facebook, at his blond curls full of sea salt, him in a swimsuit, on the beach. He's lost his decadent air and is full of iodine.

I don't know why, but people I'm afraid I've betrayed start a new life for themselves at the seaside.

Even if I didn't feel the sacred fire of writing burning within me, when I was little, for a while I kept a diary. I wasn't interested in preserving memories of my childish suffering, but in misleading my mother. Knowing she would read it—which, of course, she did—I was giving her the gift of a version of me all for herself.

Sometimes I added drawings too—since I liked to draw—including a pictorial version of a mind game I played called The Massacre, in which I imagined a bloodbath brought about by some unknown cause: people lost limbs, were drawn and quartered, coughed up internal organs. My mother saw no problem with a little girl daydreaming about a gruesome, splattered apocalypse, as long as there were no arising sexual instincts. When, thanks to my classmates, I discovered the stylized form of a dick, in my frescoes of massacres I began to hide little dicks camouflaged as other things: flowers, chimney stacks, the pigtails of a little girl sadly forced to walk on her hands because her lower limbs had been blown off and were showering down onto her dog.

A few years ago I reread those diaries, and the difference between my imagination and reality wasn't so clear: I must have worked hard to make it plausible enough that my mother wouldn't realize she'd been duped. Now, for me, that deliberate concealment was making any revelation impossible. And yet I felt a strange intimacy with what I was reading: nothing in it was true, and I was overcome with affection. They were my first steps in imposture. It crossed my mind to use some of the pages in the diaries and include them in this book, just like I thought of including letters between me and Cecilia, but apart from aesthetic intention, I couldn't see the point. I might as well invent them, I thought. They'd already been invented anyway: the diaries written just for my mother, the letters in which I talked about a senior year I'd never experienced, the ones I had Amory Blaine send me, in which he listed off his many romances, just to make me jealous.

After I gave him the first pages of my novel, my brother and I made an agreement about our two books on our family: to avoid influencing each other, we wouldn't read the other's work while writing our own. Actually, it was a unilateral agreement, because I was the only one who made it, since he, as always, didn't see what the problem was. His novel is in large part about the company where my father worked, and for months now he's been conducting interviews with former employees who knew him.

A few days ago he told me he'd interviewed Rosa. "Want to hear the recording?"

That was hitting below the belt, since curiosity was bound to win out over any fear I might have of being influenced.

We were sitting at a table on the sidewalk outside a sad-looking pizzeria, in the mugginess of an August evening in Rome. I don't know why my brother and I are so intimidated by seriousness, as though we're afraid of the momentary burden. We have a deep love for sloppiness, we need to tone down declarations of love, throw in a stupid joke, splatter sauce on the page on which we're writing something that makes us cry, leave our fly open if someone's breaking up with us.

That night my brother was wearing his usual wrinkled shirt with a button undone at his belly and one arm of his glasses attached with red tape. He set his phone down on the paper tablecloth between our plates, his empty and mine with limp pizza crusts on it. Then he played the audio recording and ate my crusts.

Rosa—whose name isn't Rosa—had a voice that was full and still young, a strong Roman accent, and a wonderful sense of humor. Since my brother intends to write a political novel, a good part of their conversation dealt with the company's unionization and the inescapable devastation of layoffs. Rosa still remembered everything from those years. She spoke about our father's role, about how he suffered when torn between his solidarity with the workers and his responsibilities as a manager.

Then my brother, in the same casual manner as he might plunk an audio recording of his father's lover down on the grimy outdoor table of a pizzeria, suddenly asked her: "So, did you and he have a love story?"

In my memory, Rosa is the woman who wrote bland love letters to my father. The truth is, I don't remember anything about those letters. I'm barely even sure they exist. I don't know if there were really three of them. I wouldn't be able to quote a single line from them, and it's not true that I recall what her handwriting was like.

In my family, each of us has our own way of sabotaging our memory out of self-interest. We've always manipulated the truth as though it were an exercise in style, the fullest expression of our identity. At times we at least give ourselves the benefit of the doubt regarding our acts of sabotage, keep within us a tiny glimmer of the truth so we can reestablish exactly how events actually occurred, but far more often the opposite happens: we forget the initial lie or the very fact that it's a lie to begin with.

For example, my mother is convinced the ring I wear on my left hand is an heirloom from nonna Muccia. It's gold with a small cameo and dates back to the transitional period between adolescence and adulthood, when girls stop wearing silver and move on to gold jewelry. I'd been obsessed with cameos.

I tell my mother I bought it on my own, and she sulks. "Why do you always have to tell me lies?" I don't know why it's so important to her to think the ring's from my grandmother, but by now I've bought into her story enough to have forgotten where I got it. When someone tells me, "Nice ring," I say it was my grandmother's. I might even hazard a nostalgic smile, as though I missed her espresso cup being slapped against my chest.

As for my father, he practiced his manipulation through despotism—that was what constructed reality, walls, and other people's wishes. To him, there was no such thing as memory, just the efficiency of the present, finding solutions to problems no one ever had. When he decided to buy my grandparents' place on the outskirts of Rome, showing up at his sister's with a suitcase full of cash, he passed the entire transaction off as the realization of everyone's dream, as the heroic salvation of his entire family, while I'd been begging him for years to buy me an apartment in Berlin back when it was cheaper than what one in a tiny village in Aspromonte would cost.

My brother, whose prodigious memory alone would've gotten him into Mensa, is afflicted by rare forms of amnesia. Once I told him about a tragicomic event in my life.

"Sounds like a scene from a novel," he told me.

It sure did.

A few years later I found that scene in his novel. I sent him a message claiming copyright.

"No way. Really? What a coincidence!" was his reply.

To me, Rosa's three letters were something similar. Today I can't tell how much of it I made up, but even back then my fraudulent processing was at work. Narratively it seemed I

had my story. I had disobeyed my father's orders, had stolen
his keys to the house, and fate had led me to the letters.

In the imagination of my twenty-year-old self, I needed
that betrayal. I didn't want to harbor any romantic illusions
about my parents. I didn't want to accept that love was represented by a depressed woman who listened to Radio 3 and
a bad-tempered man who built walls inside homes.

My brother has always seen my parents' relationship as a
model: two people who loved each other until the end. For
me it was the model of everything I would never want in
life: two people who didn't make each other happy and were
together until the end. I took Rosa's letters as the proof I was
looking for: my parents' marriage was a farce and I could feel
free from my obligations as a daughter. And I needed that
proof so badly that I probably ended up inventing it.

My mother embraced widowhood with the same stoicism
as my grandmother had. I've always hoped she'd meet someone new, that she'd let herself be taken in, that she'd find
new meaning in the word "lecherous," but I know it won't
happen. At night when I can't sleep and her multiple good-
night messages start coming in (*"Hey you, good night," "Night
night," "Good night from your mother," "Sweet dreams," "Sleep
tight," "Good night," "Good night and good luck"*), sometimes
she ends up calling me "dear," and then for a moment I de-
lude myself into thinking they weren't meant for me, that I

accidentally intercepted a message intended for a lover, and
I lie there basking in that delusion. She thinks of the army of
my never-born babies, I of the band of her never-been lovers.

Today, though, I realize that finding Rosa's letters also
served another purpose. My leaving town with Za, the ex-
citement of sneaking off, the road trip there, the yearning
desire before we arrived: I was finally about to consummate a
romantic getaway. But then what? That was the question that
made me spend the rest of the day focused on that epistolary
distraction. I was anguished by the "then."

I'm someone who goes to say goodbye to departing Russian poets and teenaged boyfriends with Bob Dylan lyrics
tucked in their pockets, but I don't go so far as to get on a bus
headed for Moscow or follow the busker down the streets of
Dublin. When Amory Blaine waited for me outside school,
he lavished me with pearls of wisdom: "The sentimental
person thinks things will last—the romantic person has a
desperate confidence that they won't." I nodded, but wanted
to be even more radical than him, to have a desperate confidence that things wouldn't even begin.

"So, did you and he have a love story?"

Rosa took a moment to reply, a moment that seemed endless as I sat there listening to the nervous silence, one halfway
between embarrassed and amused.

"I don't know, Christian. It depends on what you mean by 'love story.' What does it mean? I might know what love is—"

She paused again. She had perfect timing. The pizza crusts on my plate were all gone.

"But a story is an ambiguous concept."

Then she gave a more direct answer, but it interested me less.

My brother looked at me with self-satisfaction, as if to say, "Get a load of that!"

I never know what to do with other people's self-satisfaction. I look at it as an alien monster and then get depressed.

My brother took his phone off the table and started writing a really long Facebook post about the trash collection situation in Rome. It's one of the topics that most agonizes me. I know he started writing it only because I hadn't validated his self-satisfaction. There are two topics I've vetoed because they make me feel fragile and helpless: trash collection in Rome and the fines he has to pay.

If at age three he would try to bite into a glass when someone didn't humor him, at forty-five he writes twenty-page posts about urban leachate.

And so, while he was working on his post, I thought of another possible version of the story with Rosa.

After my father's death, I could have contacted her. A nice meeting between women. Maybe we would've chosen not a pizzeria but a café. I could describe the encounter in all its details, her walking up to me, her stride, the way she sat down, took off or kept on her sunglasses (would it be sunny?). What would she have ordered? Did she smoke? We would've ordered wine, probably, two glasses of white. I would've noticed every slightest movement, every look, every hesitation, every tic, every mannerism to chalk up to an emotional implication. I would've wondered if she glimpsed in me something of the man she had loved and lost, just as I had lost him. They say I have my father's mouth.

The wine would arrive. Would we have made a toast? Yes, but to what? To life going on, to the survivors, the surviving women. Rosa, Oca.

"I'm sorry," she would've told me.

Then I would've looked her intently in the eyes—brown? blue?—because that's how it's done, two women at a table in a café, two glasses of wine, a scene in a TV show, and I would've parted my lips, my father's mouth, to utter the words like a literary balm.

"There's no need. I'm happy you loved each other."

Then there would've been the final words, even an emotional epiphany, a tiny detail that only those who knew my father could've known. We would've spoken of all the times he lost his temper, which in hindsight ended up seeming more comical than threatening, or his shirtsleeves, which he had the tailor take in because he was so short. We would've laughed. We would've been moved. And finally, a heartfelt toast. The epilogue of every great story: reconciliation. Roll credits.

How I wish I had moments like that in my life. Telling Cecilia why I didn't go to Villa Borghese at ten in the morning. Letting nonna Muccia know that today I devotedly contemplate ragù simmering on the stove, and sometimes even cook a hard-boiled egg inside a roast. But how can you reconcile with something or someone if your memories are hazy? If they change in the very process of forming?

They can take away everything but our memories, people say. But who would ever be interested in that kind of expropriation?

Most memories leave us without our even noticing; as for those that remain, we're the ones who secretly pawn them off, traffic them, become their eager pushers, door-to-door salesmen, hucksters in search of some dupe who'll buy into our story. Dirt cheap, half off.

Memory, for me, is like the game of dice I used to play when I was little. It's just a matter of deciding whether the game is pointless or rigged.

A few days ago, a friend of mine asked me what my latest book—this book—was about. I didn't know what to tell her. Every sentence contradicted my last, every summary seemed ineffective. It felt like I was throwing together alibis, defending myself for a crime no one had accused me of.

"Yeah, but why are you writing it?" she said, as though the question would put me at ease.

The meaning behind all things tends to look the same as soon as you're asked to put it into words, and it seems like the truth might exist only in reticence. I once wrote a diary to lie to my mother, but what was I doing now?

A man whose opinion has become enormously important in my life recently told me my writing was "frosty." Since he's a writer too, he can't have chosen the word by chance. It was neither an insult nor a compliment, or even a quiet observation. It was an opinion that went beyond our literary tastes, beyond criticism, though deep down, if there's one good—or bad—thing in talking about literature, it's that it always turns out to be a pretext to talk about something else. His view was that I wasn't at all frosty in life, but did every-thing I could to be that way in my writing. I used books as a shield, dodged the most fragile, tender, and comical parts of myself. In answer to my girlfriend, I could have said, "I'm writing it for him," but now that I say it, it's as though the reasons were already someone else's.

I thought back to what Rosa had said: "A story is an ambiguous concept."

To me, writing is essentially that. I write things that are ambiguous, frustrating. Even the few fairy tales I wrote as a girl were like that. Once there was a stalk of wheat that grew in the woods.

"How'd that happen?" my grandpa asked me.

"I have no idea."

The story ended there. My grandpa was fine with that. So was I.